Thunder Above, Deeps Below

by A. Rey Pamatmat

A SAMUEL FRENCH ACTING EDITION

FOUNDED 1830

SAMUELFRENCH.COM

ISBN 978-0-573-70017-0   Printed in U.S.A.   #28061

MUSIC USE NOTE

Licensees are solely responsible for obtaining formal written permission from copyright owners to use copyrighted music in the performance of this play and are strongly cautioned to do so. If no such permission is obtained by the licensee, then the licensee must use only original music that the licensee owns and controls. Licensees are solely responsible and liable for all music clearances and shall indemnify the copyright owners of the play and their licensing agent, Samuel French, Inc., against any costs, expenses, losses and liabilities arising from the use of music by licensees.

IMPORTANT BILLING AND CREDIT
REQUIREMENTS

All producers of *THUNDER ABOVE, DEEPS BELOW* must give credit to the Author of the Play in all programs distributed in connection with performances of the Play, and in all instances in which the title of the Play appears for the purposes of advertising, publicizing or otherwise exploiting the Play and/or a production. The name of the Author *must* appear on a separate line on which no other name appears, immediately following the title and *must* appear in size of type not less than fifty percent of the size of the title type.

In addition the following credit *must* be given in all programs and publicity information distributed in association with this piece:

> *THUNDER ABOVE, DEEPS BELOW* **was supported by the Eugene**
> **O'Neill Theater Center during a residency at the**
> **National Playwrights Conference of 2008.**

> *THUNDER ABOVE, DEEPS BELOW* **received its World Premiere**
> **production with Second Generation;**
> **Gladys Chen, President; Lloyd Suh, Artistic Director.**

THUNDER ABOVE, DEEPS BELOW received its world premiere production in 2009 by Second Generation at the TBG Theater. It was directed by Pat Diamond; the set was by Sandra Goldmark; the costume design was by Camille Assaf; the lighting design was by Scott Bolman; the sound design was by The Broken Chord Collective; the production stage manager was Lyndsey Goode; and the assistant stage manager was Danielle Buccino. The cast was as follows:

PERRY	Darian Dauchan
THERESA	Maureen Sebastian
GIL	Jon Norman Schneider
HECTOR	Rey Lucas
MARISOL/BOATWOMAN	Phyllis Johnson
MR. LOCKE/PRINCE	Rafael Jordan

CHARACTERS

(in order of appearance)

PERRY, 19, African-American, a business student who assists with the books at his family's tire shop, the Prince of Tires

THERESA, 19, Filipino-American, a homeless woman

GIL, 24, Filipina, a homeless transsexual

HECTOR, 17, Puerto Rican-American, a homeless prostitute

MARISOL, 24, Dominican-American, assistant manager at a chain dough-nut shop, possibly a sorceress of some kind

with...

BOATWOMAN, ageless (to be played by the actor playing Marisol)

MR. LOCKE, late 30's, and **THE PRINCE**, early 20's, African-American and Iranian (two men in different disguises to be played by one actor)

SETTING

Chicago, various locations

TIME

Now

AUTHOR'S NOTES

Thunder Above, Deeps Below is conceived as taking place on a stage with three levels: one on the surface of the stage, one high above it, and one midway between the two. The director and designers should feel free to do it with platforms, do it with stairs, or to re-interpret it entirely and not do it at all.

Intermission should be taken at the end of Act II, with The Other Act, Scene 3 opening the second half.

While not directly adapting any source, the playwright owes consider-able creative debt to Pericles, Prince of Tyre by William Shakespeare, the photographs of Philip-Lorca diCorcia (particularly "Alice. 1988" and "Tim. 1990"), and a barista who worked in the Barnes & Noble Astor Place café from at least 1994-1996, perhaps even longer.

He, doing so, put forth to seas,
Where when men been, there's seldom ease;
For now the wind begins to blow;
Thunder above and deeps below...

    – William Shakespeare, *Pericles, Prince of Tyre*, Act I, Scene 4

The Other Act: Resurrection
Scene One

*(**PERRY** alone, high above the stage.)*

PERRY. I stepped into the water and I felt her kiss my toe. My little girl Azure loves the water. Even brisk Lake Michigan water – cold nine months out of each year. I brought her to the Lake this last April Saturday, when the water still isn't quite right and chills you to the core. A deep chill to stop your heart and set your spirit free. But Azure's spirit is already so free – she ran right in; leapt in with a squeal before I even knew what she was up to. I charged after her, visions of drowning, hypothermia, pneumonia – or at least bronchitis, a head cold, a toe cut on a sharp stone – speeding through my head. And as I ran into the Lake – even with my daughter's life in the balance and despite the sharp stab of April water – all I felt when I plunged in was a kiss, *her* kiss on my toe.

(The light ripples a watery kiss.)

And now I need to leave my daughter and the quiet western shores of Michigan and cross the lake to the bustling eastern shores of Illinois, because now I know that she is on the other side.

Please…will you help me?

*(Lights rise on a hooded **BOATWOMAN** midway above the stage. The sound of waves. A low rumble of thunder.)*

End of Scene

Act I: Confession
Scene One

(On the other side.)

*(***THERESA*** *and* **GIL** *sit on a curb.* **THERESA** *holds a coffee cup from a chain doughnut shop, "Dippin' Do's."* **GIL** *holds a cardboard sign that says: "Money for silicone. Help a girl realize his dream.")*

*(***THERESA*** *shakes the cup; coins slide around and jingle.)*

GIL. Spare some change?

*(***HECTOR*** *enters, flirting with a young woman he sees in the vicinity of the audience.)*

HECTOR. *(into the audience)* Hey, shorty.

(Shake/slide/jingle.)

GIL. Sir? Spare some?

HECTOR. *(into the audience)* Girl, what you want?

(Shake/slide/jingle.)

(into the audience) I got it.

GIL. Sir, some change, please? Some change?

(Shake/slide/jingle. **HECTOR***'s "shorty" moves on.)*

HECTOR. *(into the audience)* Oh, come on, baby, come on.

(Shorty is gone.)

(to **GIL***)* What the hell is that sign?

GIL. I don't even get a hello, *papi?*

HECTOR. Hi, *papi.*

GIL. *Ay papi!*

HECTOR. How you expect to get breakfast with that stupid-ass sign scaring everyone away?

GIL. You're stupid.

HECTOR. Don't make me blow up your spot, yo. That chicks-with-dicks stuff scares people.

GIL. Good thing I plan on getting my dick cut off, too, then.

HECTOR. Oh, oh, oh shit, yo. Oh, no man! Keep it to yourself.

THERESA. Let him have his fun.

HECTOR. What we got?

THERESA. Buck-fifty. It's Monday.

GIL. Everyone spent all their money.

THERESA. On beers.

GIL. Drugs.

THERESA. Horses.

GIL. Whores.

HECTOR. And it's a good thing they did.

(**HECTOR** *produces a small wad of cash.*)

GIL. *Jesu-Maria-Josep.* It's like Santa Slut.

HECTOR. Stop with the slut.

GIL. You just called yourself a whore.

HECTOR. It was a joke.

GIL. So this money is a joke? You blew that big-dicked man for fun?

HECTOR. Shut your cock-sucking mouth.

GIL. *Bakla puto.*

HECTOR. *(to* **THERESA***)* What did he call me?

GIL. *Maricon puto.* How's that? *Puta.*

HECTOR. I'm no queer, wonderbra.

GIL. Faggot whore. Maybe not a faggot but a faggot whore.

HECTOR. Yeah, well unless that mouth wants to wrap itself around more than some tasty dick meat today, you best behave.

GIL. "You best behave. 'Sup? 'Sup? Yo, yo, yo." I don't do that homeboy shit.

HECTOR. Then maybe I should spend my green on my homeboys.

GIL. So they can beat your skinny *puta* ass?

THERESA. Guys. *(to* **HECTOR***)* I guess he wanted a quickie before work.

HECTOR. Naw. She's away. Drove with the kids to her parents in Pennsylvania or some shit. Who the hell is from Pennsylvania? I spent the night.

THERESA. You should rethink your pricing structure if that's all you got for a whole night.

HECTOR. That's all I got for breakfast. Lunch, dinner, comics…that's coming out of here.

(**HECTOR** *produces another wad of cash.*)

GIL. God bless your cock-sucking mouth!

(**GIL** *takes the breakfast money and runs offstage [into the Dippin' Do's].*)

THERESA. Starting to sound serious.

HECTOR. What's serious? I served him. He paid me.

THERESA. Overnight. In his home. He could set you up. Get you a place.

HECTOR. He ain't gettin' me no place, a-ight?

THERESA. You can get more. You are deeply involved in his life –

HECTOR. Deeply what? He's some queer ass boyfucker, you know? I'm keeping us fed. And this is how I do it. This is how we get fed.

THERESA. I'm just saying: he gets you a place, you'd be set up, and we'd have a place to keep the stash till it's time to go. That's what's important: getting to San Francisco. Don't let whatever you feel get in the way of that.

HECTOR. 'Cause you sure as hell won't. What's with you today?

THERESA. We crashed at that squat on Clark, so I didn't sleep too well. All kinds of people there high and fucked up on so much shit I was hallucinating.

HECTOR. Let's go to a shelter tonight or some hotel.

THERESA. No, save it for food. It's warm out these days.

HECTOR. Yeah, and I'm getting comics.

THERESA. Jesus –

HECTOR. It's my money. Gil and I, we're buying comics, a-ight?

THERESA. Fine, fine.

HECTOR. He's maybe going to call me later, anyway. Wifey's pops is sick or something, so she and the kids are hanging with him till the end. Shug'd be there, too, but his job ties him down. And, you know, sometimes I do, too.

THERESA. Make sure you get more cash for that.

HECTOR. Yo, I don't need no bitch pimp, a-ight?

THERESA. We've got to be ready to go, and I feel like something is…something.

HECTOR. I feel you: you're worried, because we ain't made it yet. That's some smart shit. But I'm telling you, we ain't freezing our asses off this year. We are mos' def' going out west.

(**GIL** *enters with a Dippin' Do's bag and a cardboard coffee carrier with three cups.*)

Chow down, ladies. *Papi* is bringing home the bacon.

GIL. Bringing home the bacon, beating the meat, same difference.

HECTOR. Gil –

GIL. Choking the chicken, chomping a bone.

HECTOR. Hey, just 'cause you want a piece of this –

GIL. No, even one piece of that skanky shit is too much for me –

THERESA. You guys! Please!

GIL. She's cranky.

HECTOR. Seriously.

THERESA. GIL, LAY OFF.

GIL. *(different subject)* What are we getting today?

HECTOR. We could get lotsa different shit.

GIL. No. X-Men.

HECTOR. Yeah, yeah. That shit is crazy, with the White Queen –

GIL. No, no. The classics. I don't want crazy science fiction crap. I want classic superhero fun. Let's get a graphic novel, ha? More bang for your banging.

THERESA. You're all about heading west, and then you blow your cash on stupid comic books.

HECTOR. Yo, step off.

GIL. They're not stupid.

THERESA. They're not Shakespeare. It's a waste.

GIL. It's not your money.

THERESA. It's not yours either.

GIL. Sometimes it is.

THERESA. It's always Hector's money. Your money is for your surgery.

HECTOR. And medical dick-chopping is better than spending it on comics?

THERESA. It's a goal. For the future.

HECTOR. What future?

GIL. The future where I am fabulous.

HECTOR. You want I should be adding to my college fund or some shit? Mind my taxes? This is what we got, Trese: eat, sleep, shit, repeat. Reality. Or escape. And sometimes I use my reality to get some escape. So whatever bug crawled all up in your cunt, you best be poppin' it out, 'fore I pop you. Come on, baby baby, squeeze. Squeeze that baby back out!

THERESA. I want a real escape. From cold enveloping this town, from sleeping on trains, and from frost creeping inside my shoes and sticking to my feet.

HECTOR. What's it matter to you? You already the ice queen.

GIL. I lost my job. She's all bitch of the year, because I lost my job.

THERESA. Lost isn't exacly –

GIL. I quit it. But I had to. Nat was beating up one of the other telemarketers again, and I couldn't take it.

HECTOR. You'll get a new one.

GIL. I already have something lined up.

> *(to* THERESA*)* So stop going crazy over where we spend Hector's money.

THERESA. I'm going crazy over where we're getting your money.

HECTOR. What's the job?

THERESA. He's not taking it.

GIL. I'm going back to the club.

THERESA. That guy that –

GIL. Is long gone.

HECTOR. If he wants to go, let him. And if anyone messes with my boy –

GIL. Girl.

HECTOR. I'll take care of it.

THERESA. Because that worked out real well last time.

> *(to* GIL*)* You can't even make real money there without turning tricks.

GIL. I made it all the way from the Philippines without giving up my pow-pow for pesos.

THERESA. Well, now's a great time to start!

HECTOR. You got problems about turning tricks?

THERESA. You can take care of yourself.

GIL. First of all, that man was not a trick. He was a poor dating decision, okay? Second, I got away. He didn't rape me, did he? Third, just because it happened while I was working at the club, doesn't mean it happened because of the club.

THERESA. So explain why you quit in the first place.

GIL. I was confused, and now I'm not. And we need the money. Just because you're in charge of the stash doesn't mean we have no clue how much is there, okay? If I don't work, we're not getting out of here before the cold hits. At least, not together.

THERESA. If you end up dead in some alley, we don't go together either.

HECTOR. We go together, or we ain't going.

GIL. I didn't know you cared, Theresa.

THERESA. I don't. You made a lot of money at the telemarketing place.

(Lights change.)

*(**PERRY** enters high above the stage. He wears no shoes and his pants are rolled up to his mid-calves. He step-drags his feet, and as he does we hear the sound of water. **PERRY** crosses the space and disappears.)*

(Lights change.)

HECTOR. Yo, Trese?

THERESA. Yes, I…I'm okay.

GIL. You're shaking.

THERESA. Something is… Is something – ?

*(**MARISOL** enters from the direction of the Dippin' Do's. She wears a cheap, worn out uniform that should be cute and a severe expression. She stands tall, crosses her arms and shoots daggers at the trio.)*

MARISOL. Move down.

HECTOR. Here we go.

MARISOL. How many mornings do I have to tell you to move your asses down the block?

HECTOR. We're paying customers today.

MARISOL. Then next time you buy food, you come sit inside.

HECTOR. *¿Quieres que me venga adentro? ¿Es eso lo que quieres, mami?*

MARISOL. *No empiezes.*

HECTOR. Well, we can't collect no change in there.

MARISOL. You can't *solicit* out here, either.

GIL. Sweetie, we aren't scaring anyone away. Besides, they love us. They come here every morning expecting coffee with more buzz than crack cocaine and sweet smiles from our angelic faces.

MARISOL. The manager has been riding my ass, and he's here in half an hour.

THERESA. Let's do what the lady says.

HECTOR. Why? She don't give a shit about us.

MARISOL. You think you're too old for me to spank you, Hector?

HECTOR. Yo, I'm grown. You don't gots to watch the neighbor kid no more.

MARISOL. But I will and I got eyes in the back of my head –

HECTOR. "And old magic running through my veins!" Yeah, I remember.

MARISOL. Look: George is only coming for a half shift. You guys move on now, and I'll give you first pick of the afternoon leftovers before the shelter comes for them.

THERESA. Come on, guys. Up, up. Go to the park. Come on! Up!

(*They notice* **THERESA** *lingering behind.*)

HECTOR. What are you going to do?

THERESA. I'll catch up with you. Go.

(**HECTOR** *and* **GIL** *reluctantly obey and walk off.*)

Marisol, do you have a minute?

MARISOL. Not to loiter out here. Come inside.

(**THERESA** *and* **MARISOL** *head for the Dippin' Do's.*)

End of Scene

Act I: Scene Two

(MARISOL grabs a coffee pot and suddenly they are in the doughnut shop. THERESA sits at a table with a cup of coffee. She reveals a wad of cash.)

THERESA. Sixty dollars legal tender.

MARISOL. Quite a take.

THERESA. An overnight. He's starting to do overnights.

MARISOL. Poor kid.

THERESA. Not for long. I told him to raise his rates.

MARISOL. When his dad ran out, we all looked out for him. But you can only do so much. One time I bought him school clothes? The very next day his mom sold them for smack.

THERESA. Jesus.

MARISOL. So there are some cracks in your heart of stone.

THERESA. One or two.

MARISOL. How do you feel about Hector's overnights?

THERESA. Hector is taking care of himself.

MARISOL. But don't you wonder what it's like for him? Behind closed doors, we can only guess what happens.

THERESA. What I wonder doesn't – look, take it or don't take it. I'll worry about what I think.

MARISOL. Coffee?

(Before **THERESA** *can answer,* **MARISOL** *freshens her cup. She waves her hand over the cup with a flourish.)*

They don't mind that you –

THERESA. They don't know. They work, I panhandle and take care of the stash so no one can give it up. But it's too much to risk now. You have a safe here, you could put it there.

MARISOL. How much?

THERESA. One-oh-five, so far.

MARISOL. And what's the money for?

THERESA. Three bus tickets to San Francisco.

MARISOL. Finally ready to move on?

THERESA. I'm always ready. It's just now I have the means, if Hector and Gil don't fuck it up. You know, you could start paying us.

MARISOL. For what, exactly?

THERESA. We're like advertising. Sitting out there with the cups. Every time people spot us change they get a good look at the Dippin' Do's logo. They see the cup and think, "I could go for a cruller. An eclair." Or something.

MARISOL. Once you got some statistics to back that up, I'll tell George to figure out a fee.

THERESA. Sounds like he's still giving you a hard time.

MARISOL. He'll probably give me an even harder time if he finds a hundred and five extra dollars in the safe.

THERESA. He can't hold anything against you. You practically do his job for him.

MARISOL. He may make me miserable, but it's a good arrangement. I cover for him, he gives me extra paid time off. I can pick Manny up from school twice a week and spend more weekends with him. Raising my baby alone, it makes a difference, you know?

THERESA. Sure...I mean, I guess I don't...

(**THERESA** *is distracted. She stares into space.*)

MARISOL. Theresa? You okay?

(**THERESA** *sips her coffee.*)

THERESA. I just remembered a dream I had last night. A man waiting at the edge of the water. And this pressure on my lips like a fish swimming against my mouth. Wiggling or something. I remember...It's hard to put it all together.

MARISOL. My grandmother read dreams. A regular *bruja*, that one. Water is good. It means you're getting in touch with your deeper soul. Fishes, though. All I know about fishes is they smell bad.

THERESA. It doesn't matter. With Gil at the club again, anything could happen. If he ends up hurt and Hector ends up in juvie or with his mom, at least I'll know the cash is safe. That the whole plan won't be lost.

MARISOL. Don't you care about them at all?

THERESA. I'm not freezing out here this winter. Just take care of the money for me. For us.

MARISOL. I wonder sometimes how you ended up where you are. Did you choose this life?

THERESA. Your life is no better than mine –

MARISOL. Maybe it is, or maybe it isn't. You want to find out?

(**MARISOL** *goes behind the counter and returns with a piece of paper that she sets in front of* **THERESA.**)

THERESA. I don't need –

MARISOL. Things open up in here. I could help you. Choose something – someone else to be.

(**THERESA** *shoves the money back in her pocket.*)

THERESA. Who I am…That's for me to know. What we do, where we go, we'll take care of it. We can take care of ourselves.

MARISOL. Theresa, take the application.

THERESA. I'm going west.

MARISOL. Take the application and give me your stash.

(**THERESA** *gives* **MARISOL** *the money and takes the application. She turns to leave.*)

(*Lights change…*)

(*…as* **MARISOL** *holds up a closed fist.* **THERESA** *freezes where she stands.*)

Maybe I was wrong. Maybe you didn't choose this life. But now I'm giving you a chance to choose it or something else. You have a choice.

(**MARISOL** *opens her fist and lights return to normal.* **THERESA** *exits.*)

End of Scene

Act I: Scene Three

(Late night on the waterfront. **HECTOR** *sleeps, clutching a graphic novel, like "X-Men: From the Ashes."* **THERESA** *and* **GIL** *sit with the distant sound of Lakeshore Drive behind them. Much closer, waves lap quietly against the embankment.)*

THERESA. Water. And a kiss. I don't think it was a fish anymore. But something pressed against my lips. Something alive, but probably not a fish.

GIL. Listen to you, talking to that witch about your dreams. I didn't think you believed in magic.

THERESA. I don't.

GIL. You should. Our country was created by magic.

THERESA. Your country.

GIL. One bird got sick of flying between Sea and Sky, so she started a fight between them. The bird dodged as they hurled stones at each other, until piles of pulverized rock covered the earth – rising out of the Sea, cutting into the Sky. And then that clever little bitch, proud of the magic she invoked, rested her wings and sat her ass down on the first land: the Philippine archipelago.

THERESA. You've got to be shitting me.

GIL. Your parents never told you this story?

THERESA. Maybe when I was five. Even then I would have told them to go fuck themselves.

GIL. Do you know how I came to the States?

THERESA. MAGIC. You caught a chicken for dinner and squeezed a genie out of it's ass who granted you one wish. And you said: "I want to be in America!"

GIL. How do you spell "Theresa"? L - I - L - B - I - T - C - H.

THERESA. R - E - A - L - I - S - T.

GIL. Well, there was no genie, but it was magic. Gilbert Corazón was training to be a computer networking specialist. Even in high school she could hack the Philippine government's network. But when Gilbert's father caught her modelling dresses from Mrs. Corazón's closet for her boyfriend that life ended.

And with nothing but the dress on her back, Gilbert was on the streets of Manila. Until she started a new life through an agency that sent young ladies to the Middle East to work as housekeepers. Six months later, Gilbert was in Iran cleaning up after a wealthy family's oldest son.

(The **PRINCE** *appears high above the stage in thobe and keffiyeh.)*

THERESA. You never went to Iran.

GIL. That is how I began to work for my Prince three years ago – my distant cousin to princes, really. He was a beautiful young man with a face as smooth as mine. Two years younger than me and a poet. He was very curious about the world, and that's why we moved to America.

My Prince enrolled in the comparative literature department at Northwestern University. I came along to Evanston, Illinois – just me and him in his private condo. At this point, I still wore the hijab – the veil – to ensure he would only see my true gender and not the one my organs deceive people into believing I am. Then, one day, my Prince said:

PRINCE. You don't have to wear the hijab here. Not at all.

GIL. And because I wanted to be known as female not because of the robe, but because of my shapely hips, my supple legs, my cascade of rippling black hair…

THERESA. Okay, okay, I got it.

GIL. …I began wearing the uniform the agency provided. Until my Prince said to me:

PRINCE. You don't have to wear a uniform here. Not at all. Why don't we get you some proper clothes?

GIL. And soon I had a modest wardrobe to bring him coffee in elegant, but practical skirts. To chat with him in blouses dark enough to hide stains or light enough to tolerate bleaching. To slip out in a pink robe and pull a blanket over him when he fell asleep on the couch. Until my Prince said to me:

PRINCE. You don't have to wear a skirt here. Not at all.

GIL. I want to wear a skirt.

PRINCE. I only mean you should not pretend to be something you may not want to be, just to be my servant. My servant does not have to be a maid. My servant can be my man.

GIL. Can your man be your woman?

PRINCE. My man can be what she wishes. As long as she wants to be mine.

GIL. And then, I leaned in to him, and I kissed him.

THERESA. This is made up.

GIL. *Jesu-Maria-Josep!* How else would you explain a transsexual Filipina computer networking specialist ending up on the streets of Chicago?

THERESA. You've never told me this story before.

GIL. You've never needed it before. There is no more powerful magic than a true story told at the proper time. The right story can save a life, reveal a trickster, or reunite lovers.

THERESA. If you have a Prince, I think you'd have introduced us by now.

GIL. Well, every fairy story has a complication. Ours had a meddling cousin who came for a surprise visit and then reported back to his aunt and uncle that American decadence had corrupted their son. The little Prince was called home and, knowing that taking me back to Iran meant I'd lose my beautiful head, he left me here.

THERESA. He left you.

(*The* **PRINCE** *disappears.*)

GIL. Before he could take care of me, they froze his accounts, took his apartment. So...here I am on the street. Just like Manila. Because the only place for *bakla* is no place.

GIL. *(cont.)* But one day, he will come back for me. I held onto the maid outfit for awhile, so he would know it was me, until I realized he would know me without it. He will know.

THERESA. So you trashed it, conveniently disposing of any evidence that your tale is true.

GIL. No. I gave it to a photographer, believe it or not. He wanted to take a picture.

THERESA. If it's true, then get a computer job or something. We'd be in San Francisco in a week.

GIL. As soon as they asked for ID, they'd see my passport and ship me back to the Philippines. Besides, I can't spend my life looking back on two fathers who hate me, two countries who hate me. Here I will get my surgery. And one day, my prince will come.

(PERRY appears high above the stage where the PRINCE had been standing.)

THERESA. But he left you. It's unforgivable.

GIL. I have to believe, though. Otherwise, why put on my pumps everyday? Why beg strangers for change? Why hope at all? If I don't believe in the magic that will make it happen, I might miss my moment.

THERESA. I believe in figuring out where our next meal will come from. There's no time for stories of how the earth came to be or Princes who will never come.

GIL. Or messages delivered in dreams?

THERESA. It's not a message.

(PERRY disappears. THERESA stares into Lake Michigan.)

GIL. A dream can be magic; it's a story you tell yourself. I think you should kiss it.

THERESA. No.

GIL. Kiss the water.

THERESA. If I kiss Lake Michigan, used syringes will bob up and stab me in the mouth.

GIL. You dreamed of water, and something pressing against your lips. There is a whole world beneath those waves and it is calling to you. Touch it, kiss it, and maybe you will hear it more clearly.

(**THERESA** *gazes into the lake. She leans forward. Nervously, she lowers her head and kisses its surface.*)

(*The light ripples a watery kiss…*)

(*…And fade out except for a shaft of light over* **THERESA**'s *head. She closes her eyes and breathes deeply.*)

(*The sound of wind picking up, blowing into* **THERESA**'s *face. The sound of waves louder and faster as* **THERESA** *grips the embankment, staring into Lake Michigan's depths. She pants in fear and moans suddenly. Again.*)

(*The wind whips violently. The waves crash with thunderous impact.* **THERESA**'s *throaty moans soar among their sounds in unadulterated ecstasy.*)

End of Scene

Act I: Scene Four

(THERESA appears midway above the stage, the job application clutched in her fist. At first, only her head is lit, but as she speaks more of her becomes visible.)

(She is soaking wet.)

THERESA. How did I end up with a life like this? Is that what you've been waiting to hear? Does it keep you awake to know that I am wandering the streets digging through trash? Begging for scraps? Do you wonder how you can lay there, safe between your sheets even though I know that what happens between sheets is dangerous enough to both embrace life and give it away?

He was beautiful. The sun shone in his smile, and his eyes were lights to break fog and guide ships home. He loved me, and that was beautiful. We were beautiful.

Then one morning, I felt nauseous in Chemistry. I took a pregnancy test, and I was. Pregnant. And I don't know if I was wise beyond my years or stupid beyond belief or just fifteen, but I wanted her. I was a well-educated only child. My parents were doctor and nurse from a well-off family back home, and my Lola lived with us in the room next to mine. I could have the baby and go to college, I thought. There would always be someone to care for her, and if he wanted her, too, there were four brothers on his side, two with families of their own. We would make it with our baby of light, ready to burst forth like the sunrise. So I told my parents who the father was, and my mother said:

"You mean that black boy? I don't have a problem with black people. And his family works. It's good, they are working black people. But, Tessie, they own the gas station. In the Philippines, you would not have a baby with that family."

Then came the weeks of silent glances, my mother's whispers to Lola, my father's distant reservation... and before long it was a problem that we weren't sure about marriage and there wouldn't be money to raise her and did I know how much their adopted friend was loved by his adoptive family? Until finally my father bolted out of his chair at dinner and exploded:

"You refuse to marry. You refuse to give up your baby with a black boy, an American boy. If you want your American baby, then have it. Have your America, but not with us! Give it up, or give us up!"

...

What could I do? She was my family, he was, too. But they were my family first.

When I told him my decision, his eyes clamped shut and re-opened with darkness. There was no longer light there to guide me home. I left him. And it was unforgivable.

That final month of my life, a constant storm churned inside me. The uncontrollable flood of tears convinced me that my baby, who would be taken and given to some other family, would enter the world a shrewd and shrivelled raisin. But when she was born I saw – in that one moment as she was rushed out of the room – that she was beautiful. And then my eyes dried up. My mind shut down. My soul shut the door of this fleshy cage, crossing a barricade of arms over its chest. I embraced the silence of the dead. Everyone – mother, father, *everyone* fled my silence, as it dug its claws into their ears. And empty of her life and burying my own, I rose from my bed. I floated through the hospital in my white paper gown. I stepped into the night and onto the frozen surface of Lake Michigan. I walked away from life a step at a time across the water. Who wants it if it will not allow me that beautiful man, that beautiful girl, that beautiful family to love us all no matter how different or flawed? Or American…

(Lights come up to reveal that it is dawn at The Dippin' Do's. MARISOL has been listening to THERESA's story.)

THERESA. *(cont.)* And that is when you found me, Marisol. Sick and shivering, frost stuck to my feet.

(She holds up the application.)

That's how I know what a life like this costs – I've already paid its price. I won't do it again. That is who I am and why I'm here.

But who are you? What are you doing to us? Is it the food? The coffee? Marisol?

MARISOL. I'm not...Nothing. Here. Have a seat. Let me – I'll get you a towel. Have a seat.

THERESA. No. I...I can't. I have to go to the water. I have to go wait by the water.

End of Scene

End of Act I

The Other Act: Scene Two

(**PERRY** *alone, high above the stage. He is waist-deep in water and has not shaved or cut his hair for a few days.*)

PERRY. I ran to Theresa's hospital room to tell her my parents were suing for custody of the baby who would be our Azure, but she was already gone. I searched for clues. Who was the last one in the room? Was anything left behind? Taken away? But the trail was cold and dead, and so I thought she was.

(*The* **BOATWOMAN** *appears holding a sturdy pole.*)

BOATWOMAN. How do you know she isn't?

PERRY. Because now I know how her trail became cold and how cold it became. I see her midnight walk on frozen water, bare feet pressing melted prints with slow steps. Footprints that disappeared months later as a spring thaw pulled them apart into a million drops that spread across Lake Michigan. A trail so cold it was eaten by heat, and only remembered again in a shivered surge from big toe to hips, shoulders, head, and memory. The memory of lips.

BOATWOMAN. Then wait for the water to freeze again and for the path to reassemble.

PERRY. The footprints won't reassemble when the path does. And what if my clarity clouds over with the lake? Please – I'll pay anything – just take me across.

BOATWOMAN. A journey over water is a journey between lives, and you're already dangerously close to Death.

PERRY. Close to Death? I'm breathing, moving –

BOATWOMAN. His mark is on you: bleached bone fingers have slashed numbered scars on your soul – some black as bruises, others red like festering wounds – and He has bound them up in cream and sea green bandages.

PERRY. I buried myself in work, when she left. My dad is the Muffler King of Kalamazoo, and I keep his books. First, it was just after school, then I started taking business classes. Before I knew it, I was encouraging my dad to add a tire shop to his gas and tune-ups operation. It was a hit, and the Muffler King dubbed me his Prince of Tires.

BOATWOMAN. And now you think I can help you dig free of the work that has become your grave? Resurrection is not as easy as you think.

PERRY. Resurrection?

BOATWOMAN. There is a boatman who brings souls to Death. Is it that surprising to discover a boatwoman who performs resurrections? You aren't ready to cross; you don't even know what you're asking.

PERRY. If I'm so close to Death, it's because she's so far from me. In Death I became the man she needed. I held onto her daughter. I built the home I couldn't build before. Now I need to fill that home with her. My life…she is waiting for me on the other side. Please.

(The BOATWOMAN *considers. She holds out her hand.)*

BOATWOMAN. Step aboard.

End of Scene

Act II: Deception
Scene One

(Afternoon on the waterfront. **HECTOR** *talks to an off-stage woman.* **GIL** *absentmindedly shakes the Dippin' Do's cup, paying more attention to the graphic novel in his lap.* **THERESA** *distractedly searches the surface of Lake Michigan as she addresses unseen passersby.)*

HECTOR. *(into the audience)* Hey, girl.

THERESA. Sir.

HECTOR. *(into the audience)* It's beautiful, right?

(Shake/slide/jingle.)

THERESA. Spare some change.

HECTOR. *(into the audience)* That blue on the water, moving in waves like your hair.

(Shake/slide/jingle.)

THERESA. Spare some change.

HECTOR. *(into the audience)* But I'd take the brown of your eyes over that blue any day.

THERESA. Some change, sir.

HECTOR. *(into the audience)* Naw. I ain't no player. I'll be all yours...

(Shake/slide/jingle.)

THERESA. Some change.

HECTOR. Yours...

(Shake/slide/jingle.)

THERESA. Change.

HECTOR. All yours.

(Shake/slide/jingle.)

THERESA. Sir, please, some...

*(***THERESA*** *walks to the waterfront, still looking out at the lake.* **HECTOR***'s woman is gone. He joins* **GIL***.)*

(A bearded **MAN** *in a very fine suit and sunglasses appears behind them and observes them silently.)*

HECTOR. Don't read ahead.

GIL. You were distracted.

HECTOR. *(seeing the cup)* What we got?

THERESA. *(not looking away from the water)* Three dollars.

GIL. Bad day.

HECTOR. We could go uptown with that. But not out of town.

GIL. Not west.

HECTOR. On a cross-country bus set for San Francisco where we'll sleep in the sun. Hang in the park. Mess with artistic *chicas* that get creative on the canvas, on the page, between the sheets. Not like this shit hole Chicago.

What the hell we doing by the water? We need an area with heavy foot traffic.

THERESA. I'm staying here.

HECTOR. We gots to make our take, you hear?

THERESA. So go.

HECTOR. We're not bound to her or some shit. We can go wherever we want.

GIL. We can.

(They stare quietly at **THERESA** *for a moment.)*

THERESA. Hector…knowing what…would you have been better off if she had just left you? Your mother.

HECTOR. The hell you talking about?

THERESA. Maybe it's you. The man in my dream is searching for some woman.

HECTOR. Yo, I know which corner to find my moms at.

THERESA. Maybe she's punishing me –

HECTOR. Why would my mom punish you?

THERESA. Not your mom.

HECTOR. Who – ?

THERESA. I'm moving down a little.

(THERESA abruptly walks off.)

HECTOR. She must be having her period or something. Girl don't make sense, lately.

GIL. Show our fearless leader respect. What's wrong with you today?

HECTOR. It's almost four. He might –

GIL. Right.

(a beat)

*(**HECTOR** notices the mysterious **MAN**.)*

HECTOR. Yo. 'Sup?

*(The **MAN** nods, glances sideways at **GIL**, and exits.)*

Freak.

*(sitting next to **GIL**)*

Where were we?

*(**GIL** opens the graphic novel. They pass it back and forth as they read.)*

(as a comic book hero) "I was in love with a woman named, Jean. We were going to get married. But then... she died. I thought it was behind me. All of the grief, but all of the... joy, as well. And then I saw you. I met... you."

GIL. *(as a comic book heroine)* "But... this is me. She looks like me! Am I everything you prayed for and dreamed of, Scott? Or am I a nightmare, returned from the grave to haunt you? I don't... know what to say. I... need time to think."

HECTOR. *(as a hero)* "Of course, Maddie."

(as a thought bubble)

"This was the right thing to do – a little pain now could prevent a real tragedy later on. But then why do I feel like... I've never been more wrong? Am I trying to relive my past, resurrect something... someone better left dead? But I care for Maddie, we're having a great time. Do I just ignore everything we feel?"

GIL. Yes, Scott! Yes, you do! Because she is a clone, an evil clone who will try to take you and your baby into hell!

HECTOR. That hasn't happened yet.

GIL. Whatever.

HECTOR. *(as a thought bubble)* "I only know one thing: running away from problems never solves them."
(as a hero) "Maddie—?"

GIL. *(as a heroine)* "I'm back. Hello."

HECTOR. *(as a hero)* "Hello yourself. Ready to talk?"

GIL. *(as a heroine)* "Yes. Sorry if I frightened you."

HECTOR. *(as a hero)* "Madelyne...I really like you."

GIL. *(as a heroine)* "Because of who I am, or who I look like?"

HECTOR. *(as a hero)* "I'm not sure. But I want to find out."

GIL. *(as a heroine)* "Fair enough. Let's put in some music and start with another dance."

(as himself) I wonder what they're listening to.

HECTOR. No one gives a shit what they're listening to. This isn't some fucking teen drama piece of shit.

GIL. Oh, please. Comic books are soap opera for boys. Supposedly you want to know Magneto's or Mystique's next evil plot, but really you want to know if Rogue will ever fit in, if Jean will be resurrected, and if Cyclops only loves Madelyne because she looks like his dead lover.

HECTOR. Yo, shut up.

GIL. It's how you frame it. I can be what you see me as, or I can be what I want you to see me as. I can even be what I want to be but haven't yet become.

HECTOR. That shit's confusing.

GIL. Soap operas are confusing. So are comic books. So are you. The way you sell yourself.

HECTOR. For the millionth time, I ain't no fucking faggot.

GIL. I didn't say you were a fucking faggot, you little bitch.

HECTOR. Yes, you did.

GIL. You sell yourself as –

HECTOR. I'm not selling myself as shit, you stupid faggot, so shut your fucking faggot mouth.

(**GIL** *slams* **HECTOR** *across the face with the book and throws it at him.* **HECTOR** *sits quietly.*)

I just – you know, I can't play this game today.

GIL. The game where you pretend to hate me to hide the fact that you actually do hate me?

HECTOR. You fucking hate me.

GIL. If you feel any hate coming off me, it's because so much is shooting out of you today that it's bouncing right back.

HECTOR. I would. I would hate me.

GIL. What?

HECTOR. I would. You think I shouldn't hustle. The things I do, Gil. Who I am. The things I say sometimes when he – what I just said –

GIL. Are just words. Hector, you know who you are? A good man. A good man, who once did a very good thing for me and Theresa – for me, who is good to me and Theresa and anyone else worth being good to. That's who you are, no matter what you do.

HECTOR. What I am.

GIL. What you look like. What do I look like? Gil or Jill?

HECTOR. Gil.

GIL. But who am I really?

HECTOR. Jill.

GIL. Jill. And one day everyone will see it, and they will say, "How are you today, young lady?" They will see me for the woman I truly am just like they will see you for the good man you truly are.

HECTOR. I don't hate you, Gil. Jill. I don't.

GIL. Okay. Now, let's read more.

HECTOR. I lost our place.

GIL. Just start anywhere.

(**HECTOR** *opens the graphic novel.*)

HECTOR. *(as a hero)* "Madelyne...I like really you."

GIL. *(as a heroine)* "Because of who I am, or who I look like?"

(**HECTOR**'s *phone rings. He checks the caller ID and answers.*)

HECTOR. *(into the phone)* Hello? Yeah. Hey. What's up? Yeah. Yeah. Okay.

(**HECTOR** *hangs up and looks to* **GIL**. **GIL** *closes the book.* **HECTOR** *exits.*)

End of Scene

Act II: Scene Two

(A dining room. At one end of a grand table sits **LOCKE***; at the opposite end,* **HECTOR** *with food in front of him.)*

LOCKE. You don't have to finish it.

HECTOR. You know how it be – burgers and fries, that's me, right? This is all…what is this?

LOCKE. A calamari salad.

HECTOR. Yeah, you know, this shit's too rich for my blood or whatever.

LOCKE. Nothing's too good for my prince.

HECTOR. Yo, I'm not into that. Like you're my moms or something.

LOCKE. Or father. Daddy wants to be sure his boy is well fed.

HECTOR. I ain't no one's boy, a-ight? You better step –

LOCKE. I'm sorry. That's not – I didn't mean it like that. I'm fond of you. That's all.

HECTOR. Yeah, well, give me a few years to stop being your son, and you'll be moving on to fresher meat.

LOCKE. I won't.

HECTOR. Circle of life. I hear that. Not like I'm into this boy-fucking shit. You're the fucking perv.

LOCKE. Would you like something else to eat?

HECTOR. Naw, but, you know, I can't hang around all night this time. I got things.

LOCKE. Sure. Beer?

HECTOR. Yeah. Yeah, a-ight.

*(***LOCKE*** exits. ***HECTOR*** gets out of his chair and pokes around the room, until* **LOCKE** *returns with the beer.)*

Why you do this? You are set: this place, your girl, your kids. You rolling. So why you gotta run around and find yourself some boys to fuck with?

LOCKE. I don't fuck with boys, Hector. I fuck with you. Just you.

HECTOR. Jesus, lay off the precious moments! Man. You are one freaky-ass freak. Laying your entire life on the line so you can get a little *pinga* – I mean big *pinga*, right? It's big.

LOCKE. Oh, yeah.

HECTOR. Right. So what I'm saying is…man, I wouldn't be screwing around.

LOCKE. Life isn't just about the things you have.

HECTOR. Don't mean you act the fool and risk losing them. Or, set up with some dude? Set up, don't set yourself up, that's what I'm saying.

LOCKE. I prefer a simpler life.

HECTOR. Your life's not simple, 'cause you're a freaky-ass freak setting yourself up for a fall. You know, I know some fags…

LOCKE. (*over* **HECTOR**) I'm not a "fag."

HECTOR. (*without stopping*) …and I mean dress wearing faggoty fags…

LOCKE. Hector.

HECTOR. …but they're fucking June Cleaver compared to your faggy ass.

LOCKE. HECTOR. YOU CALL ME "A FAG" ONE MORE TIME AND THE NEXT THING YOU WILL SEE AFTER MY FIST SMASHES YOUR FACE ARE IRON BARS SLAMMING THEMSELVES SHUT IN FRONT OF YOU.

HECTOR. YO – I HEARD YOU, A-IGHT?

(*as if about to say "fag"*)

Ffffffffffffffffffff-*reak.*

(**LOCKE** *grabs* **HECTOR** *roughly by the neck and kisses him, eventually forcing tongue into* **HECTOR**'*s mouth.* **HECTOR** *tolerates it for awhile and then pushes him off.*)

Well…that was really not gay, yo. Really not gay considering you're an old dude macking on an underage hustler who's going to be packing your ass pretty soon. Really, really not gay.

LOCKE. Hector...white people are gay.

HECTOR. So?

LOCKE. White men. A black man...black men are not gay. You hear me? I have a wife, I have kids, I go to church, and I praise our Lord's name every Sunday. I've got a good job. I'm not prancing around Boystown on the arm of some white man overcompensating for his diminutive size by bulking up at the gym. I don't go to clubs or faggot bars. I don't tune in to the white faggot cable network with their queer as fuck crackers. I'm not a florist or a hair dresser or a back-up dancer for Britney Spears or whatever white bitch they're following these days. Will and Grace don't have black friends, and Damon Wayans doesn't have any queers to go with his wife and kids. I am a black man, you understand, a black man. And there is no such thing as a gay, black man.

HECTOR. You fuck with boys. A boy.

LOCKE. A thug. You ain't no one's boy. Are you a faggot, thug?

HECTOR. Hell, no.

LOCKE. That's right. Because sex with a man doesn't make you a fag, does it?

HECTOR. No.

LOCKE. Only a real man could get a thug to give it up. Daddy'll take care of your thug cock.

HECTOR. But you're paying boys to fuck your shithole. I'm just hungry and trying to get dinner.

LOCKE. Well, you got your dinner now, so go.

HECTOR. Where's my cash?

LOCKE. You got to earn the cash.

HECTOR. I want the cash.

LOCKE. Is that all you want?

HECTOR. YES.

LOCKE. You don't want to get off? You limp?

HECTOR. Fuck no.

LOCKE. A real man is always ready, right? He'll fuck whatever he can. You a limp-dicked, limp-wristed faggot
boy?

HECTOR. FUCK NO.

LOCKE. That's right. You're so full of cum, I can smell it in
your sweat. Because you're a man, like me.

HECTOR. I'm not like –

LOCKE. I can't help being so full of cum that I can't keep
it in, but I can keep from cheating on my wife. You
understand?

HECTOR. Right.

LOCKE. And I am not going to give up my life, because
some punk thinks I need his labels to know who I am.
Do you? Need me to know who you are?

(*silence*)

Good. Now. Let's run out and get you a burger.

HECTOR. No, it's okay.

LOCKE. But that's all you want, right? Dinner. Can't have
my prince go hungry.

HECTOR. I'm not…

LOCKE. What?

HECTOR. I'm…yeah. Let's – I'm hungry. Let's –

LOCKE. I'll get my coat.

(**LOCKE** *grips the crotch of* **HECTOR**'s *pants and pulls
him close.*)

A real man needs meat. Tasty and hot. A man needs
energy to go the extra mile. I am not going to keep
my man from being fed. See, thug? I'm yours. Yours.
All yours.

(**LOCKE** *kisses him.* **HECTOR** *gives in, eyes open.*)

End of Scene

Act II: Scene Three

(Late morning at the waterfront. **HECTOR** *enters with three Dippin' Do's coffees.* **THERESA** *focusses on the lake and doesn't look at him.)*

HECTOR. Where's Gil?

THERESA. The club. Getting ready for his show.

HECTOR. There's a cup of hazelnut Marisol made special just for you. It's got the "T" on it.

*(***THERESA*** takes a coffee.)*

THERESA. Another overnight, I guess.

HECTOR. Naw, regular day. I just made him give me more money. Dinner, too.

THERESA. Good.

*(***HECTOR*** hands ***THERESA*** the cash.)*

HECTOR. If you want to go to a restaurant for dinner, I can pay. I'm stuffed.

THERESA. Save it for winter.

HECTOR. Yeah, especially since the cup looks empty today.

*(***THERESA*** puts the cash ***HECTOR*** gave her into the cup.)*

What are you doing here, Trese?

THERESA. I…don't know. I really don't.

HECTOR. Because of one dream?

THERESA. Two now. Maybe three. And I don't think I was sleeping the last time. I *saw* him.

HECTOR. Who?

THERESA. The man on the water. This water, I think. Walking on the water, like I did.

HECTOR. So, you Jesus now?

THERESA. Fuck you.

HECTOR. Theresa, I need you not to say weird shit, because – I need no bullshit you, okay?

THERESA. I'm all bullshit, Hector. From the first day I showed up in this city like I had no one.

HECTOR. So, you going to go off to dreamland and leave me behind, too?

(**THERESA** *looks at* **HECTOR** *for the first time.*)

THERESA. No. I would never – I won't leave you behind.

HECTOR. Even though you think what you think about what I do?

THERESA. What I think doesn't matter. You don't have much choice.

HECTOR. I could sell shit.

THERESA. Sling, you mean.

HECTOR. You know. Yeah.

THERESA. Sure. Sell heroin, Hector. You could sell it to your mom. Or some other kid's mom, so you could screw up his life, too. You're doing what you can to make it, and you'll keep doing it and keep surviving, even if it…

HECTOR. If what?

THERESA. Never mind. It's fine.

HECTOR. Don't feed me your fucking line about I do what I gotta do, but Gil – she's got to do what you tell her to do. Why you think you can play me like this?

THERESA. I'm not playing you.

HECTOR. It's not about what's good for me or Gil; it's about what Theresa needs to get where she's going. You act like what you think don't matter. Like you don't want to get in the way of my life, when really you just stepping back so you can reap whatever shit you can from it. Your breakfast. Your bus ticket. If you ain't going to tell me what you think about what I do, at least don't act like you're respecting me. It's a front. Self-interest. You fronting everybody.

THERESA. Of course I care, but we –

HECTOR. So, what do you think about what I do? I need to know up from down right now, Trese. My whole life is lies, except Gil. And maybe you. Be real with me.

(**THERESA** *sips her coffee as she stares across the lake.*)

THERESA. I think it's wrong. I wish you wouldn't.

HECTOR. Thank you.

THERESA. But you have no way to make it. And all I can do is make sure you stay fed, and we stay alive. If it were in my power to make it stop, I would keep you with me, and not give you to that man. I would. Just like I should have kept her.

HECTOR. Who?

THERESA. My baby.

HECTOR. What baby?

THERESA. The baby I gave away. Three years ago. I thought it was the right thing to do. But it may have been – it *was* a mistake.

HECTOR. Is that why you made of stone?

(**THERESA** *nods.*)

You got to be. Me, too. He's going to ask me. Soon. To belong to him. And when he does, I'll turn to stone, just like you. That's in your power. Teach me to turn to stone.

End of Scene

Act II: Scene Four

(**HECTOR** and **LOCKE** at the grand dining table. The graphic novel lies unopened in front of **HECTOR**.)

LOCKE. Do we have an agreement?

HECTOR. Shit…

LOCKE. Language.

HECTOR. Fucking language?

LOCKE. This is business now, Hector. When you talk business, you watch your language.

HECTOR. Aw, fuck.

LOCKE. I wish it weren't business, but I know what you are, and what you really want from me. I wish you trusted me.

HECTOR. A-ight. Business. Mother bleepin' business and bleep.

LOCKE. Between two grown men.

(a beat)

HECTOR. How's your old lady doing?

LOCKE. Do we have an agreement?

HECTOR. How she doing?

LOCKE. As well as she could be.

HECTOR. Considering her hard earned grocery money is paying for some expensive dick?

LOCKE. Her father is dying.

HECTOR. What do I care?

LOCKE. You care because I care.

HECTOR. How the rugrats?

LOCKE. Fine.

HECTOR. And your job? You up for a promotion and whatnot? Advancement?

LOCKE. No –

HECTOR. How 'bout them Cubs?

LOCKE. What's your game?

HECTOR. We're talking business like grown men. Let's drink some beers, watch the game, hang for a few like men do. Instead of the boy-fucking bullshit we usually do. Excuse me – pedophilic sodomy or pederasty or whatever.

LOCKE. All right, but you won't get paid for that.

HECTOR. Aw, no: you will pay me, a-ight? No matter what we do or don't do.

LOCKE. I will if you accept the agreement. And you will satisfy me and earn your keep.

HECTOR. Hey, satisfaction guaranteed.

*(***LOCKE*** reaches out an open hand. ***HECTOR*** sees it...)*

(10 seconds.)

*(...and leaves the handshake incomplete. ***LOCKE*** patiently places his palm flat on the table.)*

LOCKE. You will have your own apartment, maintained by me. No visitors, no drugs, and no alcohol unless I bring it for you. Otherwise, you may use the apartment as you desire as long as there is one room furnished to my liking. Every Thursday, I expect you will be there awaiting my arrival. You will be shaved and showered, unless I give alternate instructions. If I wish to visit at any other time, my presence will only require fifteen-minutes forewarning. In addition, you will be given a one hundred dollar allowance for weekly expenses.

In return for my generosity, you will do as you are told. You will watch your language. You will stop inquiring about my family. You will stop challenging my choices. You will stop sharing your warped conceptions of black men, straight men, and my sexuality. I love my daughters, but I want a son. A young man to shape and to teach. And that man will be you, Hector. I will give you a home, more possibilities than anyone can offer you. More than any relative, friend, parent – father or mother.

*(***LOCKE*** reaches out an open hand. ***HECTOR*** sees it...)*

(10 seconds.)

*(…and walks around the table, takes **LOCKE**'s hand, and completes the handshake.)*

LOCKE. *(cont.)* You are my son now, Hector. Mine. All mine.

*(**LOCKE**, still seated, presses his nose to the front of **HECTOR**'s jeans and inhales deeply. **HECTOR** pushes **LOCKE**'s head back and looks him in the eyes. **LOCKE** fumbles in his pants, and throws cash on the table.)*

*(**HECTOR** stares coldly at him.)*

HECTOR. That's what you're paying for: something big enough to fill that hole between your lips, so you don't have to spew out lies just to fill its emptiness.

Maybe I'm not gonna give it to you this time.

*(**LOCKE** bolts up violently from his chair and grabs **HECTOR**, who pushes him off, roughly. **LOCKE** grabs him, and they struggle. **LOCKE** throws his arms around **HECTOR** and pulls him to the floor. **HECTOR** squirms and then realizes that **LOCKE** has stopped fighting and is just holding him – cradling him, tightly, like a child.)*

*(**HECTOR** freezes.)*

*(**LOCKE** tenderly kisses **HECTOR**'s cheek, a whimper escapes his throat, and then…**LOCKE** cries.)*

End of Scene

Act II: Scene Five

(Inside the Dippin' Do's. **HECTOR** *is on one side of the counter;* **MARISOL** *is on the other.)*

MARISOL. You, okay, baby?

HECTOR. Yeah.

MARISOL. You need something?

HECTOR. Yeah.

(pause)

Yeah. Yeah, how's my moms?

(pause)

Is she – I mean, you know – is...?

MARISOL. Is she what, Hector?

HECTOR. You seen her, right?

MARISOL. We all see her, every night. She looks like death. The living dead.

HECTOR. How she doing?

MARISOL. I don't know. We see her, baby. We don't talk to her. None of us have forgiven her for what she's done to you. She's nothing, Hector, okay? She isn't anything you want to – just don't think about her anymore. It's time to let your mama go. Let go.

(long pause)

(with meaning) Coffee?

*(***HECTOR*** *nods.* ***MARISOL*** *pours and as usual waves her hand over the cup.)*

*(***HECTOR*** *hands her a fistful of change and retreats to a table as* ***GIL*** *enters.)*

GIL. Did he pay for that? We're paying customers today, *mami.* I put on my saddest skirt and walked up the street into Boystown. Nothing gets those gay boys to open their wallets like a pathetic queen, let me tell you. Someone even gave me this little cutie!

(GIL *holds up a "new" dress in all its leopard-print glory.*)

MARISOL. That's going to look lovely.

GIL. It better. I start at the club again this weekend. You coming this time? I am fabulous!

MARISOL. I'll do my best. Here.

(*MARISOL gives GIL a blueberry muffin and a coffee.*)

You're going to need your strength. Give your admirers something to grab onto.

GIL. Oh, sweetie, today we pay.

MARISOL. Pay for the coffees. The coffees are worth paying for. Muffin is on the house.

GIL. Thank you, *chica.* You're a lifesaver. *Gracias.*

MARISOL. *De nada.*

GIL. A saver of lives, really. You! Our priestess, our goddess.

MARISOL. It's just coffee, Gil. A muffin and some very strong coffee.

GIL. Well, thank you anyway.

(*GIL joins HECTOR who is still staring into space.*)

(*to* **HECTOR**) What crawled up your ass?

HECTOR. Nothing.

GIL. Nothing.

(*pause*)

"Nothing...?" That's all I get today? How about, "Nothing, bitch?" Or, "Yo, yo, yo, let me drink my coffee, hoochie mama?"

HECTOR. I'm not feeling it today.

GIL. The sun is shining, you have a chunk of change that practically has, "San Francisco, here we come," written on it in green, U.S. Federal Reserve letters. Okay, our fearless leader has been staring into Lake Michigan like it's the eye of god, but just, "Nothing."

HECTOR. I need to think. What the hell do you want from me?

GIL. Mmm.

HECTOR. What does that mean?

GIL. Nothing.

HECTOR. Fuck you.

GIL. First an overnight. Now you need to think. Are you in love?

HECTOR. What?!

GIL. Oh, no no no. *He* loves *you.* He wants to set you up.

HECTOR. Now you're all psychic?

GIL. I guess Theresa and I will have to go to San Francisco on our own.

HECTOR. Yo, I'm going, okay? Because the thing that keeps me sane is remembering that when I'm with you guys, that's who I am. Because right now there are so many me's that I don't know – I have to hang on to that one. We're all going or we don't go.

*(**HECTOR** takes out the wad of cash and shoves it at her.)*

See, it's for you. It's all for you. For us.

GIL. I believe you. It's for us. Now put it in your pocket until we find Theresa.

HECTOR. He's got everything, you know? He can do whatever he wants. He's got all this shit, and...We're not asking for much, right? We're not fucking people up. We're begging for change so we can eat a fucking doughnut. Is that how the world works? Is –

*(The front door swings open and a bedraggled **THERESA** pulls herself through it. Her eyes are sunken and her breath heavy.)*

THERESA. Gil...?

GIL. Theresa, you okay?

THERESA. I had a dream...last night, another dream. I...

*(**GIL** and **HECTOR** bring her to a table.)*

GIL. *Hay, lentegs* – you're burning up!

THERESA. A dream. A man…the man was there.

(**PERRY** *appears high above the stage with another week's worth of beard growth. The sound of a boat moving across rough and stormy water.*)

HECTOR. Here, sit here.

GIL. *(to* **MARISOL***)* Do you have aspirin or something?

MARISOL. In the first aid kit. One sec.

(**MARISOL** *exits to the back of the store.*)

THERESA. And then I heard…

THERESA/PERRY.

"…[I]n sorrow all devoured,

With sighs shot through and biggest tears o'er-showered…"

HECTOR. Hey, Trese, just be quiet now.

THERESA. *(overlapping with* **PERRY***)*

"…He swears

Never to wash his face

nor cut his hairs;

He puts on sackcloth, and

to sea. He bears

A tempest, which his

mortal vessel tears…"

PERRY. *(overlapping with* **THERESA***)*

"…I swear

Never to wash my face

nor cut my hairs;

I put on sackcloth, and

to sea. I bear

A tempest, which my

mortal vessel tears…"

(*The sounds of a storm engulfing* **PERRY** *in rain and wind.*)

GIL. What is she saying?

HECTOR. I don't know. Her dream.

THERESA. *(Overlapping with* **PERRY***)* "And yet he rides it out…"

PERRY. *(Overlapping with* **THERESA***)* "And yet I ride it out…"

GIL. Theresa, listen to me.

THERESA. It's not a dream…

> *(***MARISOL*** returns with the aspirin and a cup of water.* ***GIL*** *takes them and gives them to* ***THERESA***.)*

GIL. Take this.

HECTOR. This is fucked up.

GIL. Then we'll take you to a shelter. Okay? Just take this.

> *(She does.)*

HECTOR. This is fucked up. Fucked up.

THERESA. He rides it out…he's almost here…

> *(***MARISOL*** looks up suddenly. She wanders away.)*

HECTOR. We got to do something big. Change things. I'm going to take care of us, okay?

GIL. Hector, let's just take care of Theresa now.

HECTOR. No. I'm going to fuck him up and take him for all he's got. I'm going to rob the bastard, and we're going to go to San Francisco the next day.

> *(Lights fade, but not before we see* ***MARISOL*** *looking up at the back of the store, directly at* ***PERRY***.)*

End of Scene

End of Act II

The Other Act: Scene Three

(Lights up on **THERESA** *laying in a cot midway above the stage. She is under a crude gray wool blanket with a damp washcloth on her feverish forehead.)*

THERESA. "And yet he rides it out."

*(***PERRY*** and the* **BOATWOMAN** *appear on either side of her, also midway above the stage.* **PERRY***'s hair is quite shaggy now, and his beard covers his neck.* **THERESA** *bolts up and stands on the cot. Her eyes burst open.)*

Perry?

(They sit on either side of **THERESA**, *as the cot becomes the* **BOATWOMAN***'s boat.)*

(Sudden, brutal thunder and gales.)

BOATWOMAN. Death sees your plan to be reborn. We should turn back!

PERRY. NO!

(Wind and lightning, quickly followed by thunder. **THERESA** *is almost thrown out as the boat lurches.* **PERRY** *catches her and clings to her.)*

BOATWOMAN. Then let her go.

PERRY. What?

BOATWOMAN. This boat was made to carry me and one other passenger. Two resurrections are too many. The boat will capsize, and Death will win you both, if you don't let her go.

PERRY. But she's my reason for resurrection.

BOATWOMAN. You have to abandon your old life to be reborn, just as you must close your eyes in order to open them. Throw her out of the boat!

PERRY. Never...

(The boat lurches dangerously.)

NEVER AGAIN!

(The boat crashes against a wave, pitches side to side.)

I LOVE HER, AND I WILL NOT LET HER GO.

(Another wave. **PERRY** *and* **THERESA** *fall forward, clutching each other, into the* **BOATWOMAN**'*s lap.)*

(The **BOATWOMAN** *places her hands over* **PERRY**'*s and* **THERESA**'*s eyes.)*

(The storm stops.)

BOATWOMAN. At last. You are reborn.

(She lifts her hands and the sun shines brightly.)

*(***PERRY** *and the* **BOATWOMAN** *disappear.)*

*(***THERESA** *sits up in the cot, soaked in her own sweat.)*

*(***GIL** *and* **HECTOR** *enter on the surface of the stage.)*

HECTOR. She's awake.

THERESA. You must close your eyes in order to open them.

GIL. At last. Her fever has broken.

End of Scene

Act III: Re-Invention
Scene One

(The opening bars of "Cherry Lips (Go Baby Go)" from the Garbage album Beautiful Garbage.* **GIL** *struts out in amazing shoes, wearing the leopard print dress from the end of Act II.* **HECTOR** *and* **THERESA** *[with the cup] follow her on.)*

HECTOR. Yo, spare some change?

*(****THERESA**** shakes the cup, coins slide around and jingle.* **GIL** *sings the Garbage song.)*

HECTOR. Some change?

(Shake/slide/jingle.)

HECTOR. Yo. Buddy – SIR!

HECTOR. Change, you fuck.

(Shake/slide/jingle.)

GIL. The men laughed and screamed and threw money and flowers at me.

*(****GIL**** sings the fourth and seventh verses of the song.)*

They even said, "Jill St. Joan! We're so happy to have our saint back!"

THERESA. People that remembered you from before.

GIL. Some people. Not him.

HECTOR. Panhandling is stupid. I don't got the skills or something.

GIL. *Hay,* it's because you look like the little brown boy that mugged them last night.

HECTOR. You're a little brown boy.

GIL. Everyone knows I wouldn't mug them. Stealing is not lady-like.

HECTOR. Yo, one of his watches fenced gets all of us west. Pick up some jewelry, his home theater system, we are

---

*Please see Music Use Note on Page 3

set.

THERESA. You're a fence.

HECTOR. I know a guy.

THERESA. The last guy you got showed up with guns.

HECTOR. This is a different guy.

THERESA. Now we're trusting your guy –

HECTOR. IT'S A DIFFERENT GUY.

GIL. And when I sang the bridge, they melted.

(GIL sings the bridge of the song.)

And I remembered. How to be…alive.

THERESA. Until someone tries to kill you.

GIL. He wasn't there.

THERESA. Maybe it'll be someone different. Like someone you rob.

HECTOR. Don't disrespect me out the side of your mouth. Bring it to my face.

THERESA. We are not good at crime. You'll end up in juvie again for nearly killing a man and then under house arrest with her.

GIL. AND BY THE END! Everyone was singing the chorus with me.

(GIL sings the first three lines of the chorus.)

THERESA. This works because it's the three of us. It doesn't work if you end up back with your mom, running out and picking up her shit –

HECTOR. "This" doesn't work if I'm Shug's cock-slave, either, does it? The only possibility for me is us in Cali-for-ni-yay. And I'm going to bring it.

THERESA. Fine: fuck it. Rob the guy, just keep me out of it.

GIL. Theresa –

HECTOR. You said yourself what I do is fucked up –

GIL. Hector –

THERESA. Rob the guy. But when you screw it up…

GIL. *Hay naku* –

THERESA. Rob an innocent guy who trusts you, who –

HECTOR. HE IS A FUCKED UP PIECE OF SHIT WHO PROBABLY GOT RICH BY BEING A FUCKED UP PIECE OF SHIT. Innocent? So fucking innocent he took my innocence, shoved it up his ass, and makes me reach up there to try and take it back. So now I will along with all kinds of other shit. HE IS NOT GOOD NO MATTER WHAT HE DOES FOR ME, HEAR?

(**THERESA** *bolts up and sways unsteadily.*)

THERESA. That doesn't mean we steal his! We…just…

GIL. ALL RIGHT, ENOUGH. Theresa, sit down before you fall over, and Hector go…stand over there. You're in time out.

HECTOR. But I –

GIL. TIME OUT!

THERESA. You're on his side.

GIL. I'm not on anyone's side. What are you doing? You can barely stand.

(**MARISOL** *enters from the Dippin' Do's.*)

MARISOL. You're scaring away the customers.

GIL. *Hay*, sorry, *mamacita.*

THERESA. *(looking in the cup)* We're almost done.

GIL. We're done. I have the money.

MARISOL. Either cool it and come inside or go down the block. Aisha is coming in today.

HECTOR. Gots to throw out the trash before the ghetto princess comes to survey her kingdom?

GIL. Hector.

HECTOR. What, now I can't even speak?

GIL. NO. You cannot. Shut the hell up.

(**HECTOR** *retreats to the edge of the stage and pouts.*)

MARISOL. *(to* **THERESA***)* How're you doing?

THERESA. The fever went down, and as soon as it did they kicked me out of the shelter.

MARISOL. It might be time to stop depending on shelters to shelter you. George finally got himself fired, and Aisha is coming in today to promote me. I'll be the manager of this very Dippin' Do's. It's a good thing for me. For Manny. For other people. Theresa.

(a beat)

THERESA. We'll move on in a minute.

MARISOL. All right.

*(**MARISOL** exits.)*

GIL. Theresa. I have the breakfast money.

THERESA. That's your money, for your surgery. Keep it.

GIL. It's our money. Last night I was someone born a man, transformed into the gender I should have been, and people were clapping. The Bang Bangkok Club is exactly the kind of magic we need to get to the pearly gates, or the Golden Gate, at least.

THERESA. I guess we'll see how long you'll put up with the delusion this time.

GIL. Hopefully, long enough for you to eat the muffin I'm buying you. Think we can stay deluded through breakfast?

THERESA. We can do better than prancing around like freaks onstage and stealing shit –

GIL. *Hay,* Theresa – how, *ha?* Tell me how a homeless transsexual can do better without turning tricks, mugging people, doing, selling, or cooking up drugs. Considering the choices we've got, we are not only making this work, we are making it good.

Some day my prince will come, okay? But not today.

*(**GIL** shoves some bills into **THERESA**'s hand.)*

Now, here's your choice for the morning. Beg strangers for pity you don't need or head in there and buy breakfast and a hot coffee so you don't end up dead.

*(**THERESA** looks at the money. She puts it in her pocket.)*

You need to let us take care of things for awhile. You take care of you.

(**THERESA** *reluctantly goes into the Dippin' Do's.*)

GIL. *(cont.)* Next!

HECTOR. So, we going to work this shit out, now she's stuffing her face?

GIL. I just told you: stealing is not lady-like.

HECTOR. We can pull it off. You and me, we'll make it so Theresa can get better in the sun.

GIL. You think I don't know how this works, Hector? I'm the tranny sidekick: no story of my own, because in this world anything more than two genders is no gender.

I've seen it before, and in that story I am no one. I am expendable.

But my story is different. It has a prince, maybe even a fairy godmother, and definitely a happy ending. I won't end up another tranny who dies helping her straight friend pull off some hare-brained scheme.

HECTOR. It won't be like that. Look, he's away to see his dying father-in-law this weekend. See? I already boosted his house keys. I got it going on all the damn time. I'm going to make this work. For us.

End of Scene

Act III: Scene Two

(**GIL**, *in her dressing room, changes into an elegant black dress and a faux pearl necklace. As she puts on a straight black wig,* **MARISOL** *enters.*)

MARISOL. Wow. Beautiful.

GIL. Sweetie!

MARISOL. Manny's with his dad, and I never know what to do at home without him around.

GIL. You need an excuse to see me?

MARISOL. First generation. I always got to be doing something productive.

GIL. Rest is productive. But if you want to work you could brew me a cup of your courage. Cream and five sugars.

MARISOL. I thought you were excited to be back.

GIL. I am. Stepping onstage is like remembering I am beautiful. The light warms my upper arms, which are always a little cold. My heels force a delicious pressure on my toes. An imperfection in my new dress scratches the skin above my right hip. Everything is more than real. But there is a dark side to it all. The lights are hot and the crowd is hot and I am hot, and then…a chill. Are they celebrating me when they clap? Or are they just enjoying a fantasy escape to a land of freaks?

MARISOL. Well, I'll be out there tonight applauding your return to the stage. Your resurrection.

GIL. I don't care how many times you deny it, you are our goddess.

MARISOL. Gil, there's another reason I came by. A man came to the store. Dark suit, sunglasses. He asked how long I'd known you. Your stage name, your real name, whether you work here legally –

GIL. Did you – ?

MARISOL. I'm no fool. A lot of my *mama*'s friends were illegal.

GIL. Did he show you a badge? I'm just a homeless girl, a –

MARISOL. No badge. He gave me a card.

(MARISOL tries to hand it to him.)

GIL. No. If they find it, they'll know you helped me. Let's keep everyone out of trouble.

Oh, my prince, why haven't you come for me yet?

MARISOL. It may not be what you think.

GIL. *Hay naku,* I've got to get out there. You have a seat, and let's get this show on the road!

(A microphone appears midway above the stage. Seats appear on the stage surface. MARISOL sits. GIL goes to the mic.)

(During GIL's act, the MAN in the fine suit and sunglasses sneaks into the audience holding a tall, red drink with a cherry floating in it. A rough man with a girlie drink.)

Good evening. Is everyone having a good time?

Life is change. Young to old, innocence to experience, man to...something more. But there is one constant we can all hold on to: love. So this is for my love, wherever you are, whoever you are with, because I will always be with you.

(GIL sings "Wonderful" from Annie Lenox's album Bare.)

(Applause. MARISOL and the MAN stand, clapping.)

MAN. Wonderful! Wonderful!

GIL. *(bowing)* Thank you. Ladies and gentlemen, have a drink, eat some nuts, smoke some butts. Ginger Candy will be out to spice things up in just a few.

(GIL steps away from the mic.)

(Lights change...)

(...As MARISOL blows a kiss. When it "hits" her, GIL trips and falls onto the MAN who catches her. MARISOL slips away.)

(Lights change.)

MAN. Beautiful performance.

GIL. Thank you. Enjoying your evening?

MAN. I'd enjoy it more if I could chat with you.

GIL. Just for a bit. I have to find my girlfriend in a minute.

MAN. How much for more than a bit?

GIL. Whatever cover you paid, that's how much.

MAN. That's not what I –

GIL. The price for that is more than anyone who asks can afford.

MAN. Are you certain?

GIL. More than a bit will cost a lifetime of devotion. And even if you're willing to pay, it doesn't mean I am. You want to take the chance?

(Through the darkness of the club, GIL tries to see the eyes behind the sunglasses. The MAN hands GIL his cocktail napkin and a pen.)

MAN. I didn't mean to…May I?

(GIL hesitates and then signs it.)

Have you worked here long, Ms. St. Joan?

GIL. Just a few days.

MAN. You remind me of someone. Is Jill your real name?

GIL. Look – you think we don't know how you people work?

MAN. I just wondered –

GIL. If you want to question me, you take off your little disguise, flash your badge, and ask your questions, okay? I don't want any trouble. I'm not making trouble.

(GIL runs offstage.)

MAN. But, Ms. St. Joan. Gi…I – !

(The MAN tries to follow, but spills his drink on his suit. He hastily napkins off and looks up, but GIL is long gone. The MAN sits and sucks down the rest of his drink.)

End of Scene

Act III: Scene Three

(**HECTOR** *and* **GIL**. **GIL** *wears a black trenchcoat, turban, and movie-star-in-hiding sunglasses. Lincoln Park sounds – coffee conversation, shopping, dog-walking.*)

HECTOR. You look like the lady with all the shoes.

GIL. Bite your tongue! She's crazy.

HECTOR. Your outfit ain't looking too sane.

GIL. I got it at the club. There might be security cameras. And someone's following me.

HECTOR. Who?

GIL. Let's just get on with it and get out of here. When do you think we can get out of here?

HECTOR. Yo, with no hitch we could be on our way by Monday. I'm glad you're finally appreciating the merits of my plan.

GIL. This plan has no merit, Hector. I need...we need to leave Chicago, that's all. Now would be a good time for us to go.

HECTOR. Then...let's go.

(**HECTOR** *produces a key. Suddenly they are in* **LOCKE**'s *apartment.* **HECTOR** *sits on the grand dining room table.*)

GIL. Dear lord, Hector...So beautiful.

HECTOR. Right? Crazy shit, yo. Mad wealth. He's at some Michigan Avenue firm that does corporate architecture and whatnot.

GIL. *(looking up)* A skylight in the middle of the floor...?

HECTOR. Yeah, it's like, when the moon is full, it comes through the roof, fills the top floor family room, shines through the glass floor and frames the dinner table. Wild, right? He's got movie screens that come down from his bedroom ceiling and play porn, and a bathroom big enough for a football team – no joke – with a sauna and a –

GIL. Are you sure we should do this?

HECTOR. He's a rich ass closet queer who'd crack you on the head if you met up in a dark alley.

GIL. Hector, when you said he was loaded, I thought he was some middle class working man, and you just didn't have perspective.

HECTOR. I gots perspective.

GIL. I see, *papi*, I am proved wrong. But...maybe we should reconsider.

HECTOR. Why?

GIL. This man really does love you.

HECTOR. But that foul piece of shit ain't shit to me.

GIL. I think you're missing –

HECTOR. Yo, yo, back up: when you didn't think loaded meant loaded, it was okay to jack his shit. Now you realize loaded actually means Lincoln Park, pie in the sky and you've got second thoughts? All the more reason his bling is the thing, a-ight?

GIL. A wife? Kids? A man with all this who could keep treating you like a ho', but instead wants to risk it all just to give you a home?

HECTOR. Not with you and Theresa. Not in San Francisco.

GIL. Are you sure? Have you asked him?

HECTOR. I don't want shit from him.

GIL. You're too old for foster care. The shelter system can't get you your diploma. Your mother is...your mother. He won't knock on your door everyday; sometimes you don't see him for weeks, and he spends all of December in Miami with his family. What this man wants to give you, Theresa and I could never give you in a million years. Stealing from him might not be –

HECTOR. You don't know, Gil. The person he wants to want. The person he wants me to be. And I don't want to know anymore neither. Don't bail on me. If you abandon me on this –

GIL. I'm not abandoning you.

HECTOR. My life is not some fun fairy tale. I don't got no prince to wait for. I don't got no happy ending. It's this, or it's being a whore in a whorehouse.

(The sound of metal clacking and sliding against metal, a door opening, and then loafers clicking on hardwood.)

Hide.

GIL. *Hay naku!* You'd think if you were a tranny, you'd avoid any hare-brained schemes – !

HECTOR. Hide. HIDE.

(GIL runs around in a panic and then slips under the table. She finds the graphic novel laying there.)

(LOCKE enters and stops in the doorway.)

LOCKE. Hector...what are you...?

HECTOR. I thought you were half way to Pennsylvania. He die before you get there?

LOCKE. No, but he's...I have to go. My head is not quite. All together. I left some things my wife wanted so... how – ?

HECTOR. You page me?

LOCKE. I didn't.

HECTOR. There was a message on that phone you gave me. But no message, you know? Like no voice, just this empty sound. No one else has the number, so I put two and two –

LOCKE. No. These wireless companies, sometimes they just –

HECTOR. Yeah, yeah. A-ight. You need help? I can get some of the stuff.

LOCKE. I'm just popping in.

HECTOR. Cool.

(LOCKE starts to go into the apartment. Stops again.)

LOCKE. I didn't give you a key.

HECTOR. You're extra –

LOCKE. How'd you get my keys, Hector?

HECTOR. I told you, I had –

LOCKE. HOW'D YOU GET MY KEYS, HECTOR?

>   (**GIL** *pops up from beneath the table waving the graphic novel and runs to* **HECTOR**.)

GIL. *Papi,* I found it!

>   (*She whacks him over the head with the book.*)

>   You think you can steal my shit? Bastard! I'm keeping this for a week now.

LOCKE. Excuse me…

GIL. Hi! Pleased to meet you. What a lovely home!

LOCKE. Hector –

>   (**GIL** *whacks* **HECTOR** *again.*)

GIL. *Hay,* bastard. We buy this book, and then he takes off with it forever. Dumbass whore. I tell him: "I am dogging you until I have it back, you skinny, flat-assed reason to make sure Puerto Rico never becomes the fifty-first state." Lucky he got your page, or I would be following his skank from here to eternity.

HECTOR. Yeah –

>   (**GIL** *whacks* **HECTOR** *again.*)

GIL. I hope I didn't damage your lock with my hair pin.

LOCKE. Hair pin?

GIL. I'm like Charlie's Angel. Just one, the first one, before he needed three. But I don't want to stand in the way of love, so I'll –

HECTOR. I'll come, too.

GIL. Oh, yes. We don't want to keep you from your family.

>   (**GIL** *kisses* **LOCKE**'s *cheeks and embraces him firmly, moving him away from the door.*)

>   My deepest sympathies, honey. Your father-in-law is a wonderful man with a wonderful son-in-law taking such wonderful care of our Hector.

LOCKE. Hector, who is – ?

(**GIL** *smacks* **HECTOR** *with the book.*)

GIL. Even though he can be a bit stupid sometimes. *Hay, sige*, see you, okay?

LOCKE. Who the hell are you, you fucking faggot whore?

GIL. No. You. Did. Not.

LOCKE. You cannot just break into my home, put on some show –

GIL. First of all, I can do anything I wish upon a star. Second, the only whore here is a skinny Latino boy and the only faggot is posturing in her Kenneth Coles. Finally, I offer my condolences. Father, son, and holy ghost – that old man is dying tonight. So put on your fairy wings, flit down to the quaker state, and get out of my face, girlfriend.

HECTOR. Gil, let's go.

LOCKE. I'm calling the cops.

GIL. Good. Turn yourself in. Maybe they'll take mercy on your child molesting ass.

LOCKE. He's a prostitute.

GIL. No cop is going to charge a homeless boy with prostitution after he was lured to a hotel with beer at the age of sixteen and then offered a hundred to whack off.

LOCKE. You think that cop will take the word of some transvestite street trash?

GIL. Well, let's march down to the Hall of Justice and find out. Meanwhile, your kids can wonder what Mr. Respected Working Man is up to while granddaddy dies.

(**LOCKE** *grabs* **GIL** *roughly.* **GIL** *pushes him off.*)

You think because I'm getting my balls chopped off, I got no *cojones*? Before you end up in jail for rape, molestation, assault, and attempted murder, walk away. We both know that this is not even what this is about.

LOCKE. And what is this about, you ching-chong bitch?

GIL. I don't buy this DL crap. You want that boy to start loving you, you better give him a reason, you toe-tapping little faggot –

(**LOCKE** *lunges for* **GIL** *again, this time grabbing hold of her. They wrestle.* **LOCKE** *pulls her down to the ground.*)

LOCKE. Son, I am going to smash that boyish grin off your goddamn painted face.

(**HECTOR** *pulls out a gun.*)

HECTOR. Get off her.

LOCKE. Hector –

HECTOR. GET THE FUCK AWAY FROM HER.

LOCKE. What are you doing?

HECTOR. Robbing your ass, you stupid fuck.

LOCKE. Hector, you don't want to –

GIL. Oh, he does. He has before.

(**LOCKE** *yanks* **GIL** *up off the ground.*)

LOCKE. Shut the fuck up!

HECTOR. GET OFF HER.

GIL. Hector, why don't you put that away, and I'll tell a story instead, okay? About a beautiful girl who sang at a club and had many admirers. One admirer smiled the brightest smile at every show, so the beautiful girl thought, what harm would there be in walking him home? She found out as the words, "FAGGOT! SLUT! WHORE!" echoed in a back alley as his fists pounded her.
She got away, but he came back. Security kept him out of the club, but he'd wait down the street. Then one night, Hector and a friend shot one of the man's kneecaps off. The police discovered that the man was attacking other transsexuals, so Hector only served a few months of juvenile detention. It's not the way the beautiful girl would have handled it, but when Hector's got an idea in his head – something to protect – he really can't be stopped. That's what Hector did. For me. You think you can stop him?

(LOCKE lets GIL go.)

GIL. *(cont.)* Hector.

(HECTOR gives her the gun.)

Like I said before, you want Hector to start loving you, give him a reason.

LOCKE. Hector, I want – I'll give you everything. Anything you want. Why are you – ?

HECTOR. Because I don't want shit from you. I'm just so tired of being so fucking hungry! I already got some-one who is father *and* mother for me. And she's more fabulous than you'll ever be.

LOCKE. I promise you: you will never be hungry again. Give me a chance.

(GIL grabs LOCKE's face.)

GIL. A regular prince, *ha?* That's what you'll be from now on. A prince among men.

LOCKE. Yes. Yes. Hector, I will be your prince.

(a beat)

HECTOR. I want two hundred a week.

LOCKE. All right.

HECTOR. And I'll fucking talk however the fuck I fucking want. And in the winter…I'm going away for a couple months in the winter.

LOCKE. And I'll be here when you come back.

HECTOR. If I come back.

(LOCKE nods.)

GIL. That's a good prince. Hector will make a man of you yet. Now, Hector, let's let the man get to his family. Let's go.

(They exit. LOCKE collapses, exhuasted.)

End of Scene

Act III: Scene Four

(**GIL**, **THERESA**, *and* **HECTOR** *at the waterfront.*)

GIL. JESU-MARIA-JOSEP! This girl tried a hare-brained scheme and lived to tell the tale!

THERESA. Barely.

GIL. *Hay*, you straight people are so much trouble. Can't you take care of yourselves?

THERESA. I admit: part of me was hoping you pulled it off.

HECTOR. Maybe if you helped out we would have.

GIL. Wouldn't it be nice if something came easy for once?

THERESA. But here we are again, wondering where we'll sleep, how we'll eat tomorrow.

HECTOR. We know where I'll be sleeping: in the arms of my owner. Come apartment hunting with me next week, T.

THERESA. You can tell him no, Hector.

HECTOR. You said you'd do anything to get me away from him, but when I gots a plan –

THERESA. There are other choices between robbing him blind and selling yourself to him.

HECTOR. I must need glasses, 'cause I don't see them. You got a choice you ain't told us about?

(**THERESA** *is silent.*)

And now she's just going to sit and stare at the water while he takes me away. I'm drowning. Something deep down is sucking me into it and I – You just sit there. This lake is going to swallow us all, and you're letting it.

GIL. You aren't making sense, *papi*.

HECTOR. Something has to change, and I...We ain't going, are we? It's a dream. He's going to take me in, and y'all are going to leave me there with him. Just like you got left, Gil. Just like Trese left her own damn baby. You one heartless bitch, T, not to tell me that was the plan all along.

THERESA. That's not the plan.

HECTOR. You left your own baby. Where? In the street? In a dumpster? With some man, so he can do whatever the fuck he want to her? Why should I believe that you ain't going to leave me, too? Fuck y'all. I'm gone.

(**HECTOR** *exits.*)

(*Silence.* **THERESA** *stares over the water, her stony face twitches, and then…she starts to cry.*)

THERESA. He doesn't – I can't…

GIL. It's not you he's angry with.

THERESA. What am I doing? I don't even know what I'm waiting for! Staring into. I dream of a bearded man floating across Lake Michigan. Not eating. Fever rising. And somehow all this sitting and I'm restless. For the first time in years I want…I WANT.

GIL. Maybe this is what your dreams wanted: for you to take time to sit and think.

THERESA. But the man, he…There is no man.

GIL. No boat.

THERESA. Just time. To look at my life and realize we need some change.

GIL. I think we could spare some change.

(**THERESA** *gets up.*)

THERESA. Let's find Hector.

GIL. I need to take some time and think myself for awhile.

THERESA. Maybe I should stay –

GIL. No. Go find Hector. He needs you.

(**THERESA** *exits.*)

(*A flash of lightning.* **GIL** *looks over the water as the sound of thunder rolls in. Another flash as the suited* **MAN** *in sunglasses emerges from the shadows midway above the stage.* **GIL** *stands to face him.*)

MAN. I didn't mean to startle you.

GIL. I thought you people were all about scare tactics.

MAN. Just because I'm –

GIL. INS?

MAN. *Persian.* INS? You think I'm INS?

GIL. Is it standard procedure to wait until your targets are alone on a dark street?

MAN. That's not what we're here for, Ms. St. Joan.

GIL. Then what are –

(*Suddenly, the* **MAN** *pulls* **GIL** *to him.* **GIL** *struggles, when the* **MAN** *plants a big, wet one on her.* **GIL** *hits him several times, reconsiders, and then kisses him back.*)

You –

MAN. Yes.

GIL. But how…? This can't be…

MAN. You love telling stories, but it's your turn to hear one. At a gallery opening in San Francisco, I saw a photograph: "Jill St. Joan, Illinois" – a still life of a shoe with an insane heel, a maid's outfit, and four familiar coins, Iranian rials. Sensing my fascination, Joey Bautista, the photographer, told me of a transsexual he met in Chicago. He even had the maid's outfit, because Ms. St. Joan decided, being homeless now, it was time that she –

GIL. Lighten her load.

MAN. And would you believe it, I knew this St. Joan, but under a different name? But I thought she'd be back home in the Philippines or elsewhere in the States or even long dead.

GIL. She wasn't.

MAN. I loved her, but why would such a beauty wait for a man that allowed himself to be taken from her? I had been drowning myself in work to forget her. I started a small press where Middle Eastern intellectuals could sound a peaceful voice through the fury of American extremism, and it was time for my press to expand. Yet that was the furthest thing from my mind. Instead, there I was, staring at this photograph, a high heel wiping away high ideals. Thinking one thing: I needed a reason that would make her want to see me again.

GIL. You don't need a reason.

MAN. But I thought of one.

(The MAN presents a manila envelope. GIL opens it and rifles through papers.)

GIL. Oh my god, this is so illegal. You'll get deported for –

MAN. They're real.

GIL. They're what?

MAN. As of one week ago, Gilbert Corazón legally entered the United States of America at the San Francisco International airport. I have a Saudi cousin.

GIL. San Francisco?

MAN. That's a work visa. I sponsored him as an employee. A computer networking specialist, at my press and website.

GIL. You're offering me a job?

MAN. If you'll have me – it. Servers, networking, building a web community…I'm not sure what I'm doing half the time.

I want to earn your forgiveness and, eventually, your affections. But how could I do that unless you came west with me? Will you? Come with me to San Francisco?

GIL. I'm dreaming.

MAN. I'm not a dream.

GIL. My Prince…I need to think about –

PRINCE. Those papers are yours. If you need them transferred to the club, I'll find a way. You taught me all about seeking a new life. And after destroying yours, I had to bring a new one back for you.

GIL. Well, looks like you were wrong about one thing, Mr. Right. As you can see, my life cannot so easily be destroyed.

PRINCE. I certainly can see that. Oh, yes, I can.

(Gentle thunder as the PRINCE and GILBERT kiss, long and slow.)

End of Scene

End of Act III

The Other Act: Scene Four

(The waterfront. **PERRY** *and the* **BOATWOMAN** *float in midway above the stage.* **PERRY**'*s beard now reaches to his stomach. His hair is long and disheveled.)*

BOATWOMAN. We made it across the rough waters. You made it.

PERRY. But what now?

BOATWOMAN. I don't know. I'm of the water, of the world out of which you are crossing.

PERRY. When there were small pieces of her trail spread over the water's surface, she was easy to follow. But now, here…she's EVERYWHERE. I'm so close to her now that I'm overwhelmed with her. I don't know where to start.

BOATWOMAN. What you need is a moment's rest…and maybe a hot beverage to sharpen your mind and recommit it to your quest.

I need to return to the Lake. You should find a cup of coffee. A simple cup of coffee can do wonders.

*(***PERRY** *steps down from the mid-level. As his feet touch the stage floor for the first time, the lights ripple a watery kiss. And then again. And again. The sound of water droplets. A light rain begins.)*

*(***PERRY** *exits in search of coffee.)*

(The **BOATWOMAN** *descends. As she does she sets down her pole, undoes her robe, pulls down her hood, sheds her costume. When she reaches the stage floor, we see that she is* **MARISOL**.*)*

End of Scene

Act IV: Death

*(The Dippin Do's. Rain drizzles outside. **MARISOL**
stands center wearing a manager's uniform. At the end
of a necklace she wears an enormous ring of keys. She
holds an envelope.)*

*(**THERESA** enters with a register drawer wearing a
Dippin Do's uniform. She counts her till.)*

THERESA. Some change?

MARISOL. What?

THERESA. In the safe? We keep running out of nickels and
quarters at the end of breakfast.

MARISOL. Come here a minute.

THERESA. I need to start the decaf.

MARISOL. I'll do the decaf. Have a seat.

(They both do.)

How're you doing?

THERESA. Good, I think. I'm doing well.

MARISOL. Is the manager making you miserable?

THERESA. No. I still have trouble getting the coffee right,
though. It seems like a lot to put in there. Like it will
be so strong.

MARISOL. The only good cup of coffee is a strong cup of
coffee. I have something for you.

*(**MARISOL** passes the envelope to **THERESA**.)*

THERESA. This is…a paycheck.

MARISOL. Of your very own.

THERESA. My paycheck. My…I'm not really sure what to do
with it.

MARISOL. After work we should go open you a bank
account. But you need an address for that.

THERESA. The halfway house let's us use theirs.

MARISOL. Or you could use Hector's.

THERESA. My paycheck. It's a lot.

MARISOL. Actually, it's not, but I'm more than happy to let you keep thinking that until it all comes into focus.

THERESA. So I just put all my money in the bank for a few months.

MARISOL. Well, not all. You have to eat.

THERESA. And then Hector and I head off to San Francisco. Or, at least, I...It's kind of amazing. A new way of doing things.

MARISOL. A new life. On a piece of paper.

THERESA. Thank you, Marisol.

(There is a tapping on the door.)

(seeing who it is) I'm sorry. Let me go finish –

MARISOL. I've got the decaf. Let him in.

*(**MARISOL** exits. **THERESA** unlocks the door and **GIL** enters. He is dressed in a modest, new [actually new, this time] dress. **THERESA** returns to counting out her drawer.)*

GIL. Good morning! How is the queen of the crullers?

THERESA. *(showing him the check)* Not bad. Look at this.

GIL. *Hay,* congratulations! Welcome to the machine.

THERESA. Shut up.

GIL. I'm serious. There's nothing Filipinos like more than capitalism, except maybe college degrees. When are you going for that?

THERESA. One step at a time. Besides, you should talk.

GIL. Girl, night school for me. I've got all kinds of new technologies to catch up on.

*(to **MARISOL**)* Good morning, *mami.*

MARISOL. *(from offstage)* Morning, Gil.

THERESA. So, I guess you're all packed.

GIL. Packed? I've got a duffel bag with panties, an extra pair of shoes, two skirts, two shirts, and some stockings. I'm not getting paid yet, honey. It took two seconds.

THERESA. It's very exciting.

GIL. But sad, too. We'll still meet in San Francisco, but it's not the adventure it was supposed to be, is it? I mean, look at Hector: that's sad.

THERESA. Haven't seen him.

GIL. *Hay,* you're hysterically blind. Out the window. That's him. The orange hoodie.

THERESA. Sitting in the rain.

GIL. All morning, probably. He's soaked.

THERESA. He can come in. I'm sure Marisol will –

(MARISOL enters with a coffee urn and starts the decaf.)

MARISOL. Of course he can.

GIL. I tried talking to him on the way in. He wouldn't even say hello. A happy ending for everyone, but not the one we were looking for, I guess.

MARISOL. You want some coffee, Gil? The regular is ready.

GIL. Hit me, Madame Manager.

(MARISOL serves it up. GIL puts down some cash.)

THERESA. It's on me.

GIL. When I can pay, I pay. Besides, I owe the Dippin Do's corporation at least twenty cups, probably more.

MARISOL. Keep your money.

GIL. Keep your coffee.

MARISOL. If you insist.

GIL. You give it to me, you're going to have to start giving it to everybody.

MARISOL. Honey, if I could, I would. Besides, Theresa made this pot. Test it and see if she's learned to make it as good as me. For her.

GIL. Manipulative bitch, give me the coffee.

(She does. GIL sips.)

MARISOL. So?

*(A beat, then…***GIL** releases a sigh of great pleasure.)*

GIL. Oh, Theresa, it's good.

MARISOL. Right?

GIL. Oh, sweetie, so good that I see the road opening before me – the friendly skies yawning wide to welcome me to a new world.

MARISOL. She's a quick learner.

THERESA. And don't you forget it.

(A quiet tap, just slightly louder than the rain, on the door. **GIL** *opens it.)*

GIL. Hello, stranger.

*(***HECTOR*** strides in and walks to the center of the room, the hood of his shirt pulled over his head. He also wears entirely new clothes, but they are not so modest. In fact, he is rather dressed up, in a Rocawear, Ecko Unlimited, Triple Five Soul kind of way – and far more thuggish than he would probably prefer.)*

*(***GIL*** pulls ***HECTOR****'s hood down.)*

You should take that thing off, you're soaked –

*(***HECTOR*** pushes her off roughly.* **GIL** *totters on her heels and falls over. We see for a moment that* **HECTOR***'s eyes are red from crying, until he pulls the hood back up.)*

*(***HECTOR*** takes out a gun and points it at* **THERESA***.)*

HECTOR. Give it to me.

THERESA. Give what to –

HECTOR. Everything in the drawer and the stash. Give me the stash.

THERESA. You stupid fuck.

HECTOR. Shut up, Theresa. Give me the money.

THERESA. Here's a prime example of why we aren't good at crime. We know who you are. We can call the police.

HECTOR. You really that low? To turn me in?

THERESA. If you're low enough to hold me up at gun point.

HECTOR. I knew y'all were fucked up bitches, but I didn't know you were traitorous bitches.

GIL. *Papi,* let's all sit and talk about this –

HECTOR. I'm never talking to you again. You turn on people and –

GIL. Hector –

HECTOR. SHUT THE FUCK UP, and I promise not to track your prince down and turn your fairy tale into a nightmare. Keep yapping and all bets are off, a-ight? Give me the money, Trese. I know it's here. Where else could you keep it? Give me the stash.

GIL. *Our* stash. Whose the traitorous bitch now, *puta?*

HECTOR. SHUT UP!

GIL. Put that damn thing down and tell me what the hell is wrong with you.

HECTOR. I can't talk to the dead. And you two, you left me. Shooting you would be nothing, because you're already dead to me.

GIL. Well, I must say: I'm one hot mama for a dead girl –

(**HECTOR** *shoots a coffee urn. Steaming hot coffee begins to spray onto the floor.*)

THERESA. I'm not going to die, Hector. Not now.

HECTOR. Then give me the stash.

THERESA. I've actually got a little bit of something now. And part of that something is you.

HECTOR. I ain't got shit. YOU FUCKING HUNG ME OUT TO DRY. Left me with that man –

THERESA. I told you not to go with him. I'm working here for us. We're taking the money I make and the money you make, and we're going out to San Francisco to join Gil.

HECTOR. Bullshit. You're leaving me behind.

THERESA. Never, Hector.

HECTOR. You already did! I don't let him keep me – what then? Gil flies the friendly skies, you sleep warm and cozy at that halfway house *for women*...and me? I be right where I always was: on the cold, hard Chicago concrete. Alone.

HECTOR. *(cont.)* I get y'all now. Acting like I matter, but just till something better comes along. A better proposition, a better prince, a better scheme. Y'all had something to go to. I don't, and you saw that, and you left me, covered me in shit while you shoveled your way out of it. Of course I went to him, what else was I supposed to do? Y'all left me.

GIL. Nobody left you.

HECTOR. For the last time, you better shut the fuck up, Gil, okay? You especially. You didn't only abandon me, you fucking threw me to the wolves.

GIL. That wolf can give you more than we ever could.

HECTOR. DOESN'T MATTER. NONE OF IT MATTERS. I'M ALL I'VE GOT. And I'm taking care of me. Now, Theresa. Give. Me. The stash.

(**MARISOL** *steps in front of the gun.*)

MARISOL. You're asking the wrong person, *caballero.*

HECTOR. This ain't about you.

MARISOL. It's my store.

HECTOR. *Mama, échate p'atrá.*

MARISOL. *Dame la pistola, Hector.*

HECTOR. You want to make this about you? That what you want?

MARISOL. *Quiero que te calmes.*

HECTOR. You think I forgot? You the first one who ever left me. With her. Manny comes along and suddenly you don't got time for me no more.

MARISOL. You grew up, Hector. You think I forgot? The four year-old boy I'd babysit after his *papa* abandoned him, and his *mama* had to sweep floors at the chicken place? You think any of us forgot the nine-year-old we gave our old clothes, so he could go to school while she stayed home and started selling her body? You think we forgot the thirteen-year-old man we'd invite over for dinner when she started selling her food stamps to buy dope?

HECTOR. Don't fucking pity me!

MARISOL. I won't pity you. I *don't*. But I won't forget your life. And I know you won't either.

(**MARISOL** *grabs the barrel of the gun.*)

HECTOR. STEP BACK.

MARISOL. Hector…

HECTOR. I'm going to blow you're fucking brains out. I'm going to shoot and –

MARISOL. *Papi…*

HECTOR. I'm going to. You left me, too. All of you. You're nothing!

MARISOL. Let it go.

HECTOR. All of you. I –

MARISOL. Let it go.

HECTOR. I…

MARISOL. Let go.

(**HECTOR**'s *hand is shaking, but he lets the gun go. He collapses in sobs, falling into the puddle of coffee.*)

(**MARISOL** *passes the gun to* **THERESA** *and kneels on the floor. She puts* **HECTOR**'s *head in her lap and pulls his hood down.*)

HECTOR. *Perdòn. Ay, perdòn.*

MARISOL. *Ya, ya.*

HECTOR. *Perdòn, mami. Por favor.*

MARISOL. I know.

HECTOR. I don't know what else to do.

MARISOL. Of course not. This is what life gave you. I know. I remember your life. I can't forget. But this life…this is all it can give you. So let it go. Gil and Theresa love you, Hector. They haven't left you behind on purpose. It was just their time to be reborn. But do you know how they became reborn? By abandoning lives that would do them no good anymore. They had to die. You must close your eyes in order to open them.

(MARISOL lifts her hand – wet with the coffee on the floor – and places it over HECTOR's eyes, closing them.)

MARISOL. *(cont.)* He isn't the best man in the world, but he cares about you. He can take care of you if you want, in your death. Stay with him or don't; it doesn't matter. What matters is that it's your time, Hector, to journey away from this world. Let go, join Death on his boat, drift across the water. Ripple by ripple pass along its surface as His boat pulls you away. You must let go for there's much to do in your death. As you drift, all the things you don't need from this life, drop them off the side of the boat. One by one. Watch them disappear. Sink into darkness. Swallowed by the deeps below. Then eventually, you'll see another shore. A new place. A new life.

And when it's time for you to be reborn, I will be here. On the shore waiting for you. With something warm to fill your belly, and a cup of hot coffee to start your journey back to life. I'll be here. But for now…

(MARISOL takes her hand off of HECTOR's eyes.)

(to GIL) Take him to his apartment.

GIL. Come on, *papi.*

HECTOR. I'm sorry, Gil. I'm sorry, Theresa. I am.

THERESA. Don't you be sorry to anyone.

GIL. You died today, Hector. It's our day to be sorry for you. But I know when you come to join me in San Francisco, you will be alive again. I know it.

THERESA. Get some sleep, Hector. I'll come by and see you after work.

GIL. *(to THERESA)* And I'll stay there till you arrive, so I can see you before I get on the plane.

(to MARISOL) Bye, *mami.*

MARISOL. Good-bye, Gil. Until we meet again.

(GIL leads HECTOR out. MARISOL grabs a mop and starts to clean the floor as THERESA watches her.)

THERESA. Your grandma isn't the only *bruja* in the family, huh?

MARISOL. You better start another pot of regular. The breakfast crowd gets in soon.

(**THERESA** *takes the shot coffee urn and exits.*)

(**MARISOL** *finishes cleaning and then gets rid of the mop. As she closes* **THERESA**'s *register drawer…*)

(**PERRY** *enters. His clothes are not quite so shabby, and, though he hasn't shaved in a week or so, his beard does not reach his stomach. He stands dazed in the doorway.*)

PERRY. Hello.

MARISOL. Good morning. Let me guess: coffee?

PERRY. Please.

MARISOL. It'll be about ten minutes.

PERRY. Oh.

MARISOL. But you should wait. You won't find a better cup of coffee anywhere in Chicago.

PERRY. Okay. Sure. I've got plenty of time.

MARISOL. *(yelling offstage)* Hey, step on it. Someone's waiting out here.

(**THERESA** *enters with a new urn and starts the regular.*)

I'll start bringing out the doughnuts.

(**MARISOL** *exits.*)

THERESA. Okay.

(to **PERRY***)* Sorry, I just need time –

(**THERESA** *sees* **PERRY**.)

End of Scene

End of Act IV

The Other Act: Scene Five

(Lights change. The sound of rain increases in intensity, as the drops grow in size and frequency.)

*(***THERESA*** steps out from around the counter.)*

(Intensity of the rain rises. A low rumble of thunder.)

*(***PERRY*** and ***THERESA*** slowly walk toward each other.)*

(Thunder rolls in as raindrops grow to the size of basketballs, falling into dangerously flooded streets.)

*(***PERRY*** and ***THERESA*** stop face to face. He kneels in front of her and takes her foot.)*

(Thunder pounds as boulders of water fall and crash, smashing into a newborn ocean of itself.)

*(***PERRY*** takes off ***THERESA****'s shoe…)*

(Falling. Crashing. Smashing.)

(And then the loudest crack of thunder in the history of the universe, so loud it propels immense vibrations over the water, ripples whose movements are felt across the globe, as…)

*(***PERRY*** kisses ***THERESA****'s toe.)*

End of Scene

End of the Other Act

End of Play

OTHER TITLES AVAILABLE FROM SAMUEL FRENCH

EDITH CAN SHOOT THINGS AND HIT THEM

A. Rey Pamatmat

Drama / 2m, 1f / Interior & Exterior

Three kids — Kenny, his sister Edith, and their friend Benji —
are all but abandoned on a farm in remotest Middle America.
With little adult supervision, they feed and care for each other,
making up the rules as they go. But when Kenny's and Benji's
relationship becomes more than friendship, and Edith shoots
something she really shouldn't shoot, the formerly indifferent
outside world comes barging in whether they want it to or not.

"Utterly sincere and winning drama about three good kids that
sparkles with moments of gentle comedy. Pamatmat's strug-
gling but goodhearted young characters are neither disen-
gaged nor cynical, and they feel all the more real for it."
- *Louisville Courier Journal*

"Edith... is a beautifully rendered portrait of three young
people as they struggle to remain young in a circumstance
that forces them to have the stresses of the adult world."
- *Cincinnati Examiner*

OTHER TITLES AVAILABLE FROM SAMUEL FRENCH

PHOENIX

Scott Organ

Comedy / 1m, 1f

When Bruce and Sue meet four weeks after an uncharacter-istic one-night-stand, Sue has this to say to him: one, I had a great time with you that night and two, let's never see each other again. Thus begins a 4,000 mile journey well beyond the confines of their carefully structured worlds. Bruce is fueled by an overwhelming but undefined compulsion to join her in Phoenix. Sue is reluctantly charmed by his persistence, but steadfast in her resolve to keep him at bay. Both are forced to consider a whole new world of possibility, though not one free of difficulty and loss. A dramatic comedy about courage.

"A good time...it seduces you even when you know better...rich, anxious subtext...the actors banter and play and flirt...allow your-self to get intoxicated by the pleasures of...romantic comedy."
- *The New York Times*

"Remarkable...Organ's dialogue is witty and quick, dialogue is humorous without ever sounding forced...as the play progresses, the issues these characters have about life, death, work and com-mitment reveal themselves in sometimes funny and sometimes poignant ways. The play as a whole is extremely funny, even though the characters find themselves in serious situations. The script always stays genuine to the characters and what they're go-ing through, however, and never sacrifices the work for a joke."
- *LEO Weekly*

OTHER TITLES AVAILABLE FROM SAMUEL FRENCH

ELEPHANT SIGHS

Ed Simpson

Comedy / 5m

Not long after moving to the small town of Randolphsburg, PA, uptight lawyer Joel Bixby is invited by Leo Applegate, an avuncular fast food connoisseur, to join a group of townsmen who meet in a ramshackle room at the edge of town. Leo has chosen Joel as a replacement for the late - and greatly beloved – Walter Deagon. Despite protesting that he's just not an organizational man, Joel fi nds himself mesmerized by Leo's ebullient manner and agrees to drop by - without ever asking just what exactly it is the group actually does. Determining that the meeting will at least help him network with potential clients, Joel arrives, hoping that the group's purpose will eventually become clear. Joel's confusion only increases as, one by one, he meets the group's surviving members who includes Dink, a perpetually gleeful little man who deeply loves his bald-headed wife and who is "in touch with his feminine side"; insurance man Perry, a former minister in the midst of a painful crisis of faith; and Nick, a volatile contractor who has recently lost his job and family and is desperately looking for some kind of miracle. As an increasingly anxious Joel is swept up in the strange lives of the guys, he struggles to fi gure out exactly why they've all come together. The more time he spends with them, the more apparent it becomes that each of them are just as lost as Joel. As the evening progresses, however, the regulars - and newcomer Joel - grapple with their own disappointments, offer comfort to each other, and, in the process, fi nally reveal the mysterious reason for their gathering. A group of delightful characters highlight this comedy about loss, loneliness, and the healing power of friendship.

OTHER TITLES AVAILABLE FROM SAMUEL FRENCH

MAPLE AND VINE

Jordan Harrison

Dramatic Comedy / 3m, 2f / Multiple Sets

Katha and Ryu have become allergic to their 21st-century lives. After they meet a charismatic man from a community of 1950s re-enactors, they forsake cell phones and sushi for cigarettes and Tupperware parties. In this compulsively authentic world, Katha and Ryu are surprised by what their new neighbors - and they themselves - are willing to sacrifice for happiness.

"Piquantly funny, cleverly executed and darkly playful."
- *The New York Times*

"Jordan Harrison's Maple and Vine does everything a good play should do. It entertains. It makes you think....1950's conformity may not differ much from 2011's, but at least we have our conveniences. Harrison makes you weigh the costs and benefits of both eras without hitting you over the head with his own conclusion. You will enjoy reaching your own."
- *Theatre Louisville*

OTHER TITLES AVAILABLE FROM SAMUEL FRENCH

LIONS

Vince Melocchi

Dramatic Comedy / 9m, 3f / Interior

It's the 2007 NFL season and the Detroit Lions are on a winning streak— unfortunately out of work steelworker John Waite is not. Withhumor and humanity, playwright Vince Melocchi offers a glimpseinto The Tenth Ward Club, where the patrons place their hopes ontheir team, and attempt to escape the creeping demise of their city and of their way of life.

"Lions is a drama that speaks directly to our country's current state of affairs, which is to say it's a play about unemployment, hardship and economic collapse. If that sounds like a depressing thematic lineup, the play itself is far from being a downer. Lions takes an unsentimental look at a ravaged cross-section of present-day Detroit and tells a story of compassion in a cold climate....Melocchi's play is a smart, humanistic...observation of working-class survivalism."
- *Los Angeles Times*

"Lions is about hope...about the endurance of a middle class getting squeezed...finding life amid the lifeless"
- Drew Sharp, *Detroit Free Press*

"...an all-around touching portrait of Middle America, a reminder that 'real Americans' need not be so reductively characterized as Joe the Plumber."
- *L.A. Weekly*

OTHER TITLES AVAILABLE FROM SAMUEL FRENCH

BACK BACK BACK

Itamar Moses

Drama / 3m / Interior

Edgerton Foundation 2008 New American Plays Award

Before headlines blazed, before the Mitchell Report and ESPN lit up millions of television screens with the scandals, before congressional jaws dropped, comes the story of three guys making their way in the world of professional baseball – a world too competitive to rely solely on raw talent. This explosive play from the acclaimed writer of The Four of Us and Bach at Leipzig takes you behind the headlines into the locker room to witness an even more gripping confrontation you didn't see on TV, as these teammates face each other and do battle – for their careers, their legacies, and the future of America's favorite pastime.

CPSIA information can be obtained
at www.ICGtesting.com
Printed in the USA
BVOW06s2040030217
475296BV00008B/27/P